DR. MORELLE ELUCIDATES

In *Dr. Morelle Elucidates,* Dr. Morelle expounds on seven puzzling cases in his inimitable manner. For *The Case of the Man Who Was Too Clever,* the doctor and his assistant Miss Frayle investigate the murder of an actress, whose dying screams are the clue to her death. Whilst in *The Case of the Clever Dog,* a murder is committed in the doctor's presence, but man's best friend is the clue in finding the killer . . .

ERNEST DUDLEY

DR. MORELLE ELUCIDATES

Complete and Unabridged

LINFORD
Leicester

First published in Great Britain

First Linford Edition
published 2010

British Library CIP Data

Dudley, Ernest.
  Dr. Morelle elucidates.- -
(Linford mystery library)
1. Morelle, Doctor (Fictitious character)- -
Fiction. 2. Detective and mystery stories,
English. 3. Large type books.
I. Title II. Series
823.9'14–dc22

ISBN 978–1–44480–419–5

Published by
F. A. Thorpe (Publishing)
Anstey, Leicestershire

Set by Words & Graphics Ltd.
Anstey, Leicestershire
Printed and bound in Great Britain by
T. J. International Ltd., Padstow, Cornwall

This book is printed on acid-free paper

1

THE CASE OF THE MAN WHO WAS TOO CLEVER

One evening Doctor Morelle had been visiting a scientist acquaintance who resided in a block of flats which the Doctor has sardonically described as 'reminiscent of native cliff-dwellings'. Miss Frayle had accompanied him on his visit, and they had said 'Goodnight' to their host and were descending the staircase from the second floor on their way out. As the distance down was so short they did not bother to call the lift. Suddenly Miss Frayle was shocked and horrified to hear the sound of what appeared to be a woman screaming.

The screams came from a flat on the first floor, and the creature sounded as if she were in great agony.

Miss Frayle turned a white face to the Doctor and grasped his arm.

'Doctor, listen! That awful screaming — ! It's some woman — !'

'I was not under the impression it was the squeaking of a mouse!' he replied, pausing, and glancing along the passage leading to the flats.

'It's coming from that flat along there!' gasped Miss Frayle, stepping forward as if to hurry in the direction she was indicating. 'It must be someone in terrible pain — '

The Doctor's eyes narrowed speculatively. He walked quickly past her, speaking to her over his shoulder.

'I think perhaps it would be advisable to ascertain the reason for such distress.'

She caught up with him and was saying breathlessly: 'Perhaps we can do something — ' when there came the humming of the lift ascending. The lift-gates opened with a slam and the hall-porter shot out, his eyes popping, and rushed after them.

'Here's the porter,' Miss Frayle told the Doctor unnecessarily, for he had already observed the man's approach. 'We'll go in with him.'

'Blimey! Who's kicking up the song-and-dance?' he gulped as he joined them.

'It's from the flat along here,' she said.

The screams continued, and they hurried in the direction from whence they came.

'Fancy practising scales this time o'night!' exclaimed the porter with an attempt at heavy-handed humour.

Doctor Morelle turned his head and eyed him with extreme disfavour. 'I feel fewer abortive attempts at misplaced humour and more imperative action is indicated!' he snapped.

'Something awful's happening, I'm sure — ' cried Miss Frayle as she ran alongside in order to keep up with the Doctor's raking strides, the porter was breathing stertoriously as he laboured after them.

Suddenly the screaming subsided, dying away into moans. Then silence.

'She's chucked it now, anyway!' grunted the porter. 'Flat nineteen it sounded from. That's Mr. and Mrs. Collins — '

They reached the door that bore the number nineteen, and the porter produced his passkey. There came no sound from within the flat as he turned the key in the lock.

Doctor Morelle and Miss Frayle found themselves in a small hall with a small glimpse of the lounge beyond. Chromium, glass and light oak predominated. There was a faint smell of perfume pervading the atmosphere. As the porter stood uncertainly in the entrance to the lounge there came a rapid movement and a youngish man appeared, wearing a blue silk dressing gown. His face was ghastly.

'Mr. Collins!' exclaimed the porter.

'Thank heavens — ! Thank heaven, you've come!' the man cried.

'What's happened?' Miss Frayle said. 'We heard — '

'My wife — !' was the agitated response. 'Locked herself in the bathroom! She — she's — ' he broke off incoherently, and they followed him as he rushed back the way they had come. The bathroom was at the end of a short passage on either side of which two bedrooms faced each other.

'Blimey! We'd better bust the door in!'

said the porter as Collins rattled vainly at the lock.

'Diana! Diana!' he called, and turned to them frantically. 'We must get in!' he gasped. 'Something's happened to my wife! Something's happened to her!'

'Let's shove together. Come on, sir,' addressing the Doctor, 'and you, Mr. Collins.' Doctor Morelle murmured: 'No doubt our combined efforts will prove efficacious!'

'Yes — ! Yes — !' babbled Collins.

Miss Frayle stood aside as they rushed at the bathroom door together. The door was not built to withstand such vigorous treatment, and when the three of them charged at it the second time there was a sound of splintering wood.

'Once more!' shouted Collins, and after the third attempt the door crashed open.

'Kindly remain in the bedroom, Miss Frayle!' Doctor Morelle said over his shoulder, as he caught sight of the crumpled figure of a woman on the bathroom floor.

'Better get a doctor!' grunted the hall-porter.

'Fortuitously,' murmured Doctor Morelle, 'I happen to be one — I am Doctor Morelle.'

The man shot him a surprised look. 'Oh? Lucky you was passing! Even though it's a bit too late by the look o' things!'

Collins cried; 'The key's on the floor. Diana must have locked the door before she — she — !' He broke off and knelt down beside the woman. 'She's — she's dead!' he muttered brokenly.

She was dead, the Doctor saw at a glance. Thoughtfully he stooped to pick up the fragments of a broken tumbler, which had apparently fallen from the dead woman's grasp. He sniffed at the pieces, then carried them into the lounge.

'Miss Frayle, perhaps you will kindly occupy yourself by finding something in which to wrap these fragments?' As she took them he added: 'Possibly you may have noticed the aroma of poppy about them?'

'I was wondering what it was,' she said sniffing.

'The poison which the unfortunate woman drank from the tumbler is undoubtedly laudanum — opium pre-pared in spirits of wine. Hence the aroma of poppy.'

'Was it suicide — ?' Miss Frayle began to ask, and then gave a sudden exclama-tion of pain. 'Oh! I've cut my finger on one of these bits of glass.'

'Tck! Tck! How careless of you! Let me observe the extent of the damage.' He examined the cut.

'It's nothing much.'

'Quite a superficial injury. Nevertheless it would be wiser to bandage the wound. I can use my handkerchief as a temporary measure.'

'Oh Doctor, it seems a shame to spoil it.' But in spite of her protest, he produced his handkerchief from his breast pocket and proceeded to bandage the cut finger.

'How neatly you've done it!' Miss Frayle smiled up at him admiringly, as he finally tied the knot. 'And so quick.'

'Quite comfortable?'

'Beautiful! Thank you so much, Doctor. Er — may I have it back please?'

'Um — ?' He seemed to be deep in

thoughtful contemplation of her hand.

'My hand — you're holding on to it!'

He appeared to snap out of his musing.

'Ah yes! I was momentarily somewhat preoccupied. I was considering one or two questions I wish to put to Mr. Collins. Perhaps you would be good enough to acquaint him of my identity — if the porter has not already advised him — and ask him to come here. Just call him out of the bathroom, no need for you to venture inside.'

Miss Frayle shuddered in agreement and went out of the lounge to find Collins.

In a moment he came in and sat dejectedly in an armchair, his head between his hands. Miss Frayle observed him with pity and glanced at the Doctor who was contemplating him with a look of calculation. Poor man, she thought, it must have been an awful shock to him. Surely the Doctor could leave the business of questioning him till later?

The porter appeared and poured a glass of whisky for Collins, but the latter, however, decided he didn't need it. The porter continued to hold the glass and took an occasional sip himself.

Doctor Morelle leaned negligently against a radiogram. He lit a cigarette thoughtfully.

'What — what could have happened — ?' Collins turned to him with a haggard face. 'Why should she do such a thing?'

The Doctor shook his head. 'The circumstances point to the fact that your wife died from the effects of laudanum poisoning, Mr. Collins,' he said quietly.

'Poor lady, what a shocking business!' muttered the porter, and Miss Frayle noticed that he consoled himself with another sip of whisky.

Collins suddenly stood up in a distracted manner and began to pace the room.

'I never dreamt she'd — she'd take her own life!' he cried. 'You see, we'd quarrelled — Diana was temperamental — she was an actress on the films and radio — imagined and exaggerated all sorts of things — and when she slammed out of the bedroom, I didn't take what she said about committing suicide seriously.'

'She threatened to commit *felo-de-se*?' put in Doctor Morelle softly.

'Yes. But as I say, I thought she was just being melodramatic. I called out to her something to that effect, as a matter of fact, then went to bed. As you see I'm in my dressing gown.'

'I had already observed that fact.'

Miss Frayle gave the Doctor a quick look and saw that his face wore an enigmatic expression.

Collins went on, speaking jerkily:

'And then suddenly I heard her screaming in terrible pain. I got out of bed, rushed to the bathroom, but the door was locked — '

At that moment the telephone rang in the hall. Collins broke off with a frown. He made as if to answer it himself, then turned to the porter. 'Will you see who it is?'

When the man had gone, Doctor Morelle murmured:

'Please continue, Mr. Collins. You were describing how you hurried to the bathroom and found the door secured on the inside.'

'Well, there's not much more to tell. I tried to force the door but couldn't, and — and — well, the rest you know.'

The porter returned. He said to him:

'A lady to speak to you, sir. Wouldn't give no name,' the other's frown deepened. He hesitated and then moved towards the hall. 'Perhaps I'd better answer it,' he apologised, and went out. He carefully pulled the door after him, but Doctor Morelle made no attempt to overhear the conversation on the telephone; on the contrary, he stood with his head slightly on one side, his eyes narrowed thoughtfully.

'What is it, Doctor?' began Miss Frayle in a hushed whisper.

He waved her into silence. She and the porter stood staring at him wonderingly. Suddenly he gave an exclamation of satisfaction.

'Ah! The almost imperceptible sound of some mechanical device in motion,' he said.

'Eh?' grunted the porter.

'Whatever do you mean?' asked Miss Frayle.

11

Doctor Morelle, who had moved from the radiogram to the centre of the lounge, waved his hand casually.

'I should imagine it emanates from that radiogram.'

He crossed to it with a swift movement and raised the light oak lid.

'H'm . . . As I had imagined, the turntable is still in motion.'

'So it is,' exclaimed the porter. 'It hasn't been switched off — !'

At that moment Collins returned and saw them by the machine. He paused in the doorway, then came forward eyeing them somewhat suspiciously. The Doctor turned to him with a bland expression.

'I was admiring your radiogram,' he said suavely.

The other nodded. 'Yes . . . It was a present to my poor wife She was very fond of the radio, naturally.'

'The — ah — deceased also possessed a comprehensive selection of gramophone records,' continued the Doctor, indicating a number which had been placed on a chair by the cabinet. He was turning them over as he spoke.

'You goin' to play us a tune, Doctor?' muttered the porter in a somewhat censorious tone. 'I must say it don't seem quite the moment — '

Collins cut in, his voice high-pitched: 'What's this all about? What's the radiogram got to do with my wife's suicide?'

Imperturbably the Doctor observed:

'This seems to be a somewhat unusual record.' He had picked up a disc that bore a plain white label. He glanced at the inscription cursorily. An expectant silence had fallen. Miss Frayle, who had given Collins a quick look, heard Doctor Morelle murmur as if speaking to himself: 'It might be interesting to hear this played . . . '

'This is fantastic!' Collins protested, stepping forward. 'Horrible!'

The Doctor seemed not to hear him. He was about to place the record on the revolving turntable when there came a shout.

'Leave that record alone! Put it down — !'

The next moment the disc was almost knocked from his hand as Collins made a sudden lunge. Miss

13

Frayle gasped with sudden apprehension as she saw the look on the man's face. The porter, too, gave an exclamation of surprise, but reacted quickly and grappled with him. There was a fierce struggle, but the porter's weight soon told. Collins was forced back and subsided, breathing heavily, into an armchair, with the porter standing over him, dour and menacing. As if nothing had happened to mar the equanimity of the proceedings, Doctor Morelle placed the record on the turntable and adjusted the volume control.

It proved to be an excerpt from what was apparently a highly dramatic playlet. But what caused the porter's jaw to drop and Miss Frayle to goggle from behind her spectacles was the part where a series of piercing screams issued from the radiogram.

'Blimey!' said the porter hoarsely. 'Why, that's Mrs. Collins, and them's the screams wot we heard outside!'

'Exactly the same voice — !' gulped Miss Frayle.

'A voice raised from the grave, is it not,

Mr. Collins?' said Doctor Morelle. 'And accusing you!'

★ ★ ★

'Yes . . . ' Doctor Morelle mused through a cloud of cigarette smoke, 'It was patently a clear-cut case!' He gave a thin smile of self-satisfaction, and went on:

'Mrs. Collins had undoubtedly succumbed as a result of laudanum poisoning, but the drug had been administered by her husband. How exactly the police will ascertain as a result of their examination of the culprit.'

He was sitting before his desk in the study of the house in Harley Street. It was some time later; Collins had been removed by the police summoned to the flat, and he, accompanied by Miss Frayle, had returned home.

Miss Frayle asked:

'But how did the poor woman come to be found locked in the bathroom?'

He regarded her with what he imagined was an expression of extreme tolerance.

'For the simple reason,' he explained

15

carefully, 'that the husband had dragged her there. He had thereupon locked the door on the inside and made his exit through the window to the fire escape, closing the window after him. It was a simple manoeuvre to return to the flat through the front door. In point of fact, he aroused my suspicions somewhat in the first instance by his manner of drawing attention to the key on the floor. A shade too obviously performed, it occurred to me. Whereupon I took the precaution of ascertaining if there was easy egress from the window. That was merely a minor indicative that all might not be what it purported to be, however.'

Miss Frayle duly obliged by looking at him questioningly, and he went on:

'The major clue which attracted my attention was one very obvious fact which would have been apparent to any student with the most elementary knowledge of first-aid!'

She wriggled uncomfortably under the reproach implied in his tone.

'Well, I once took a course of first-aid, Doctor,' she said, making a somewhat feeble attempt not to appear intimidated.

'Then I can only presume, my dear Miss Frayle, that even your superior intelligence had failed to absorb the fundamental fact that laudanum is a narcotic which induces a condition of painless stupor!'

She blushed, fiddled with her spectacles, and stammered:

'Why yes — Yes, of course! I remember now — '

'It followed, therefore, the wife would never have screamed out as she was supposed to have done.' He flicked the ash from his cigarette.

'Why did he deliberately attract attention by playing a record of Mrs. Collins screaming like that?' Miss Frayle asked.

'His purpose was to establish a somewhat subtle alibi. He calculated that on hearing the screams the hall-porter would rush to the scene and find him attempting to force the bathroom door — '

'You mean the way we did?'

'Precisely. Thus adding colour and credence to the story he had prepared. It would appear Mr. Collins transferred his affections elsewhere. As his wife, however, was in possession of considerable wealth which would become his upon her demise, he decided to precipitate her death in order to be in a position to embark upon a second marriage.' His nostrils quivered with repugnance. 'A sordid sequence of events, culminating inevitably in tragedy and disaster.'

'Was it the — the other woman who 'phoned?'

He nodded. 'I understand it was his inamorata.'

Doctor Morelle puffed at his Le Sphinx.

'Umm . . . ' he mused, 'were I proposing to include this in a collection of tales of — ah — ratiocination, I should be inclined to entitle it 'The Man who was too Clever'.' He gave a thin smile of self-satisfaction. 'Yes . . . a singularly appropriate title.'

Miss Frayle frowned. 'Oh, but surely, Doctor,' she corrected him after a moment's thought, 'he wasn't clever enough?'

He closed his eyes with a painfully elaborate sigh.

'That will be the subtle implication conveyed — to the discerning reader!'

'Well,' she persisted obstinately, 'I don't see how anyone can be too clever and not clever enough all at the same time.'

He replied, his voice grating with growing irritation: 'The operative word in my last observation happened to be the word, 'discerning'!'

The implication sank in and she challenged him with:

'Meaning, I suppose, that I'm not?' It was her turn to sigh, only there was nothing forced about it. Her sigh came from the heart. Then she shrugged her shoulders. 'However,' she said, 'no doubt I should be grateful to you for thinking I can read at all!'

'I confess I often suspect it is largely a matter of guesswork on your part!'

But she was determined not to be defeated this time. With what for her must have seemed to have been an inspired riposte, she flashed back at him: 'Rather in the same way that you guess at these clues you talk about . . . eh, Doctor Morelle?'

His eyebrows shot up. This was unlike Miss Frayle. For one fraction of a moment his face almost registered surprise. Then, with eyes narrowed but in a voice smooth as silk, he murmured:

'Except that *I* always happen to guess correctly, my dear Miss Frayle!'

Miss Frayle subsided.

2

THE CASE OF THE
CLAIRVOYANT CAPTAIN

Doctor Morelle paced the study with long, raking strides as he dictated to Miss Frayle. He seemed studiously unaware of the presence of a young man with a spanner who was repairing the central heating apparatus in a corner of the room.

Inexorably he intoned as Miss Frayle's pencil coursed over her notebook:

'The happenings in a single day often form a loosely-related — and even disjointed — procession of incidents. Invariably these incidents present an apparently insoluble problem, be it sociological or criminal. By collating the facts as they present themselves to an intelligent observer, the complete solution to the problem will be apparent. Paragraph — '

He broke off in deep cogitation as he gravely considered his next spasm of erudition. Meanwhile the young man with the spanner stopped tinkering with the radiator and gazed open-mouthed at him.

'I say, Doctor — ' he suddenly burst out as though he couldn't help himself, 'that certainly is a great thought. Would you say that the same applies to medical diagnosis?'

'With certain qualifications, I would reply in the affirmative,' Doctor Morelle deliberated absently. Then he halted his pacing abruptly, realising it was ostensibly a plumber who had asked that question. He gazed unbelievingly at the stalwart young man. Then he said crisply:

'While I appreciate the intelligent interest you have shown in my exposition of scientific ratiocination, I would, nevertheless, be obliged if you would not interrupt. I would prefer a little more application to your plumbing duties, and a little less loquaciousness, if you do not object.'

'Sorry, Doctor,' the young man apologised, and gave a charming grin. He was evidently a very irrepressible young man. He smoothed a hand through his dark hair. 'As a matter of fact, I'm not a plumber.'

The Doctor raised his eyebrows and his mouth tightened in irritation.

'Then what are you, may I ask?'

'I'm a medical student.'

'A medical student — how interesting!' the Doctor spoke in a tone of utter boredom. 'And am I to assume that you are labouring your way through University via my central heating mechanism?'

'Hardly that. You see, I happened to be in the shop when the young lady — ' he grinned affably at Miss Frayle — 'She'll be Miss Frayle, I imagine? Well, I heard her telephoning and the plumber found he couldn't send anyone today, so I thought I'd come and help you out.' He tapped the radiator proudly. 'I've fixed it all right.'

'Thank you for your resourcefulness. Since your task is completed there is no reason for your sojourn here to be prolonged. Good morning to you!'

'Wait a minute, Doctor,' the young man smiled again disarmingly. 'I know it was a dreadful cheek barging in like this, but I had to see you. I've written twice a week asking for an interview, and I've tele-phoned about a hundred times — '

Miss Frayle goggled at him through her spectacles.

'I know! You'll be the young man who signs himself 'Harry Page',' she said with a spontaneous smile.

'Right first time,' the young man grinned.

The Doctor clicked his tongue impa-tiently.

'This is insupportable,' he snapped 'While my amanuensis and this impostor are discussing the ludicrousness of per-sonal nomenclature, I am apparently expected — '

'Sorry, Doctor! Don't mean to be a nuisance.' The young man moved nearer.

'Nevertheless, that is precisely what you are. You deliberately put me under an obligation to you and then presume — '

'But I just had to talk to you,' the other

persisted. 'You see I've read everything you've ever written; your 'Study in Ratiocination', 'The Criminal versus Society' . . . everything. I admire you tremendously, Doctor. I think — why, I think you're the greatest man in the world!'

A smile of self-satisfaction flickered over Doctor Morelle's lips. 'While your modest appreciation of my efforts is most gratifying, I fear that you are nevertheless expending my valuable time.'

'Oh no,' the young man protested. 'I want to help you. You see I want to model my life on yours, and I thought I could work for you, to get in a little practice so to speak, and perhaps take some of the dirty work off your shoulders. You must have lots of cases you can't handle yourself, and I'm sure I could — '

'You could carry on with my intricate and highly specialised practice, leaving me quite free to pursue my hobbies of fencing and the habits of crustacean life?' the Doctor finished, with thinly-veiled sarcasm. 'Is that what you imply?'

Page grinned. 'Not immediately, anyway,

25

but I'm sure there are some cases I could handle.'

The Doctor walked to the door and opened it meaningfully.

'Miss Frayle will make a note of your invaluable offer,' he said briskly. 'We have your address, no doubt, and should an opportunity arise — which I very much doubt — we will communicate with you. Good day.'

'Good day, Doctor Morelle, and good day, Miss Frayle,' the young man enthused. 'Thanks a lot. Sorry to have barged in, and if ever — '

The Doctor had already closed the door on the effervescent Harry Page.

Miss Frayle looked at him reproachfully.

'Need you have been so abrupt, Doctor?' she protested. 'I'm sure you hurt his feelings.'

'Impossible! That young man's insensitiveness to snubs and sarcasm is unique,' he pronounced, and he lit a Le Sphinx with impatience. 'In future I wish you to examine closely the credentials of people whose presence in the house becomes essential through domestic or other reasons.'

'Very good, Doctor.'

'And now, if I may be allowed to collate my thoughts without further ebullient interruption, we will proceed with the dictation of my lecture. At what juncture did we arrive, Miss Frayle?'

' — 'the complete solution to that problem will be apparent'!' she quoted flatly.

'Oh yes.' He drew at his cigarette, and began to dictate again:

' 'Elucidation of problems which hinges purely on neurotic behaviourism presents a more — '' he broke off as the doorbell rang.

'That'll be Mrs. Jepson.'

'Inform her I cannot receive her.'

'But she has an appointment. She's been sent to you by Professor Stenhart.'

'To be sure,' he nodded. 'An interesting case, I believe, of a rather complex character. Kindly transcribe those notes in the laboratory.'

Miss Frayle pouted disappointedly. She was suffused with curiosity about this 'complex' case.

'Don't you think you may need me, Doctor?' she ventured.

'I think not. If I do so, I will ring,' he said, and observed obliquely: 'Strange how I am positively enveloped with offers of assistance today!' He stubbed out his cigarette. 'Pray announce Mrs. Jepson without delay.'

Mrs. Jepson entered the study and advanced towards Doctor Morelle with quick, nervous steps. She clasped his right hand in anxious gratitude.

'Doctor! Thank heavens you could see me!' she exclaimed in a strained voice. 'I'm sure you are the only person in the world who can help me.'

'I will endeavour to be of every assistance,' he murmured. He regarded her through half-closed eyes. A sensible, matronly type, he decided. Well-to-do, clothes in good taste. A woman not prone to hysteria, or who would exaggerate trivial worries. That she was exceedingly worried was most evident from the harassed set of her features, and her manner of smoothing her gloves.

'Professor Stenhart informed me you

wished to consult me on a rather complex matter concerning your daughter,' he said softly. 'Apart from that, I am not cognisant with the facts of the case. Pray acquaint me with the relevant details.'

'Very well . . . But first of all I'd like to ask you a question.' She leaned forward and clasped her hands tightly. 'Do you recognise any scientific basis for clairvoyance — and have you any sympathy for clairvoyants personally?'

Doctor Morelle brought the tips of his fingers together.

'While I recognise the possession of clairvoyant powers by certain persons,' he said weightily, 'I cannot at the same time condemn too strongly those charlatans who prey upon the credulity of human nature.'

'Good,' Mrs. Jepson said quickly. 'That's exactly what I wanted to hear. You see, Doctor, my daughter is excessively credulous, and she is absolutely dominated by a person who professes to be clairvoyant. I'm quite powerless to do anything about it. My daughter simply won't listen to me.'

'She prefers to listen to this clairvoyant?'

'Exactly! Everything *he* says must be right.'

'So the clairvoyant is of the male sex?'

'That's what makes it worse.' The woman pulled at the fingers of her gloves. 'Captain Zolta is — well, he's a *roué*. He's handsome in a dissolute sort of way, and just the sort of man with whom young impressionable girls would become infatuated.'

'I understand. A moment while I ring for my assistant, Miss Frayle — that is if you have no objection to her hearing the details?'

Mrs. Jepson shook her head quickly.

'My assistant is a typical example of feminine credulity,' he explained. 'She has doubtless heard something of this — er — Captain — '

'Zolta,' Mrs. Jepson prompted. 'Women are simply flocking to him, Doctor; and not only stupid girls, but women with money — Lady This and Lady That.'

He inclined his head. 'I fear,' he murmured, 'that neither an aristocratic title nor financial advantages are necessarily synonymous with common sense!'

Miss Frayle at that moment appeared through the doorway. She had run from the laboratory when she heard the Doctor's ring signalling her to his presence. She was thinking triumphantly. 'There! He couldn't do without me after all.'

'You rang for me, Doctor?'

He rose. 'Yes, close the door.' He bowed imperceptibly to the seated woman. 'This is Mrs. Jepson — Miss Frayle, my assistant.'

'Good morning.'

'How do you do.'

Doctor Morelle sat down again. 'Mrs. Jepson is somewhat anxious as a result of her daughter's association with a certain Captain Zolta — '

'Captain Zolta?' Miss Frayle echoed quickly. 'You mean the amazing clairvoyant man?'

'You see . . . ?' He turned to the woman with his hands held out palms upward. 'My assistant, as I anticipated, is an expert on such trivia.' He turned a sardonic smile of encouragement upon her. 'Proceed, my dear Miss Frayle, and communicate to me all of which you are aware concerning this fascinating — er — gentleman. Bearing in mind, of course, my age and this lady presence!'

Miss Frayle goggled behind her spectacles.

'Well Doctor, I don't know Captain Zolta at all,' she began, 'not personally, I mean. I've just heard of him, and read about him.'

'Apparently he has attained some prominence in the press?'

Mrs. Jepson said: 'Of course the cheap newspapers are bound to have written him up!'

Doctor Morelle looked at Miss Frayle with a mixture of surprise and severity, and said: 'It comes as something of a disappointment — I might say almost a shock, to learn that you, Miss Frayle, subscribe to popular journalism.'

'Well, I — I sometimes — '

'I had in my innocent way elevated your mental faculties to a slightly higher plane,' he continued relentlessly. He sat back in his chair with an air of pained resignation. 'However, continue with your sordid narrative.'

'I — I only *happened* to read about him,' she excused herself in embarrassment. 'I — I didn't — oh, well, anyway, I thought he sounded a most remarkable person. He can foretell the future just as if — as if it's already happened . . . ' She checked her enthusiasm. 'But why is Mrs. Jepson worried about her daughter?'

Mrs. Jepson said immediately: 'My daughter is completely under Captain Zolta's influence. I've no control over her at all. It's 'Captain Zolta says I must do this, Captain Zolta says I must do that' . . . She's only a young girl, and I don't like her being dominated by such a creature. It's — it's sinister. It's making her ill. I'm frightened all his mumbo-jumbo nonsense may well affect her mind. She is a bundle of nerves as it is, and she used to be such a steady, sensible girl.'

'It certainly seems most regrettable,' the Doctor observed. He gazed at the ceiling in thought, and with his gaze still turned upward, he asked: 'Have you sufficient cause to state definitely that your daughter is not only mentally dominated by the man, but that she is *infatuated* with him, and if so exactly how intricate is this entanglement?'

The other raised her hands desperately. 'Heaven only knows! I feel — feel that I don't trust my daughter any more.'

'Oh, how awful!' sympathised Miss Frayle.

'She sleeps with this wretch's photograph under her pillow and some nights she has secretly left the house to meet him. I don't know whether she has contracted a *liaison* with this man or whether she intends to, but I'm certain there is every danger. The man's intentions are so thoroughly dishonourable, and he has such an uncanny power over credulous women that even a self-respecting girl might — ' Her voice became shrill with anxiety. 'Doctor, you must help me!'

While Doctor Morelle pondered gravely, there was heard the banging of a door somewhere in the house, and excited voices. Miss Frayle jumped to her feet, and at the same time the study door was flung open. Her fears were justified — it was another gatecrasher, though this time it was a young woman.

The young woman closed the door behind her and stared accusingly at Mrs. Jepson.

'I thought I'd find you here,' she burst out excitedly. 'How could you humiliate me in this way — ?'

Mrs. Jepson walked across to the newcomer, and tried to put her arm round her shoulders, but the girl shook her off.

'Hilary darling, don't you understand it was for your own good,' Mrs. Jepson murmured consolingly.

'For my own good!' the other echoed scornfully. 'Why can't you let me lead my own life?'

Her eyes widened challengingly as she glanced at all of them in turn. She said peremptorily: 'Well, since I'm here you may as well listen to what I've got to say.'

Doctor Morelle lit a cigarette. It seemed the erudite sanctuary of his study was going to change to a bedlam for a domestic fracas. 'This is your daughter, I presume?' He drew at his cigarette.

'Yes, I'm Hilary Jepson.' She stood, feet set apart determinedly, and her gloved hands placed defiantly on her hips. There was plenty of character in the firmness of her mouth — more than a waywardness. She was evidently the type of person who has the characteristics of independence and individualism so strongly developed that she would be certain to take any course of action that was forbidden to her. Everything she did would be in the nature of reaction.

'I suppose Mother's been telling you a pack of lies about Captain Zolta and me Doctor,' she challenged.

'Your mother has been explaining about the Captain's clairvoyant activities,' he acknowledged guardedly. 'Apparently he is a most remarkable personage . . . '

'He's a wastrel and a fake,' interrupted Mrs. Jepson.

'You see . . . ? Mother's never seen the man, and yet she condemns him.' She went on slowly, 'Captain Zolta is a superman, Doctor. I think it a privilege that I should know him.' She paused. 'This morning he made me the happiest girl — he — he asked me to marry him.'

Mrs. Jepson leapt to her feet.

'He — *what*?'

'Asked me to marry him! There — !' with a triumphant smile, 'doesn't that prove he loves me?'

'But Hilary — you wouldn't — you couldn't — a man so much older than yourself.'

'I told him I'd marry him as soon as he liked!'

'Hilary!'

The girl faced her mother squarely. 'We're going to Scotland tonight immediately after his séance. We shall be married by special licence.'

'You can't do this! I forbid it!'

'Sorry Mother . . . I'm afraid you're not in a position to do any forbidding I'm twenty-one and I've control of my money.' A softer tone came into her voice now. 'Oh, Mother, why must you be against me all the time? It — it doesn't make me happy to do anything that you disapprove of, but I know I'm right.

You're so old-fashioned. Because Captain Zolta is a genius instead of some dull young man with a conventional job, you think — '

'I won't listen,' exclaimed Mrs. Jepson frenziedly. She turned to Doctor Morelle in desperation. 'Won't *you* talk to her?'

He stubbed out his cigarette. He gazed into the young woman's eyes almost mesmerically. In a low even voice he said:

'Miss Jepson, as you so succinctly expressed it, all of us are behoved to make decisions for ourselves. That is the basis of free will. To what extent one must sacrifice the pursuance of what appears to be the correct course of action to the desires of others, is purely a matter of individual conscience.'

Hilary Jepson gave a flashing smile of triumph. 'You see, Mother. Doctor Morelle's on my side,' she declared.

'Indeed, no. My attitude is quite impartial. My information as to Captain Zolta is at the moment based on the veriest hearsay. I would wish to encounter the gentleman myself before I formed a decision.'

'Now that's downright common sense,' the young woman affirmed keenly. 'I'm not ashamed of the Captain. I'm proud of him. I'd like you all to meet him. As a matter of fact, you could come to his séance this afternoon, and then you'd see what a wonderful man he really is.'

Doctor Morelle inclined his head. 'I think that might be the wiser course — that is if you are agreeable, Mrs. Jepson?'

'I'm completely in your hands, Doctor,' was the murmured reply in a defeated tone.

'That's fine,' Hilary Jepson enthused. 'The séance is three o'clock at 24, South Fanshaw Street, Mayfair.' The girl walked to the door. 'See you then — cheerio, everybody. I'm dashing off to have lunch with the Captain!'

Miss Frayle goggled after the departing young woman, and Mrs. Jepson moved to Doctor Morelle as soon as the door was closed.

'Doctor, don't you feel we're, well, cheapening ourselves by meeting this man?'

'As I perceive it, there is no other course of action.'

'But what is your object?'

He paced the room, his eyes half closed. 'Judging the case scientifically, from a psychological standpoint, our obvious course is to discredit this man in the eyes of your daughter. Then, when she sees him for the charlatan he may well be — to declare to Miss Jepson that she is at liberty to enter into a marital union with him should she so still desire!'

'You mean give our consent even when we've proved he's a rotter — ?' echoed Mrs. Jepson incredulously.

'Precisely! Under those circumstances, we could be assured that your daughter would then sever all relations with the Captain!'

Mrs. Jepson pulled on her gloves.

'It all sounds a little enigmatic to me. I hope you're right, Doctor Morelle.'

He continued his pacing, and it seemed as though he was clarifying his thoughts by speaking them aloud.

'To discredit the Captain may not be facile,' he pondered. 'There is the slight chance he might be a genuine clairvoyant. Then we would be compelled to prove he was a philanderer, which would take time. Superficially it is not evident that he is marrying Miss Jepson merely for her inheritance. No doubt a man who has such a wealthy following has ample financial returns of his own.' He stopped his pacing. 'A moment, Mrs. Jepson, while I summon my secretary.'

'I'm here, Doctor!' chirped Miss Frayle from a corner of the room.

'Indeed — ! Your presence was not observed since your powers of articulation seemed to have deserted you,' he observed dryly. 'However, it is probably just as well. Now. Miss Frayle, kindly turn your cretinous interest in daily journalism to good account by telling us whether Captain Zolta ever produces spirit materialisations. Does he produce voices through trumpets, and ectoplasm, for instance?'

'I've never heard of him doing so.'

'A pity! Such phenomena, when fraudulently contrived, would be comparatively simple to expose. Captain Zolta confines himself to predictions about the future, which are probably so vague that one might not be able to disprove them with certainty, I gather?'

'Yes, Doctor, they say he tells fortunes wonderfully,' Miss Frayle nodded eagerly.

'Hm. The elucidation of this problem portends to be complex — probably the most complex case we have ever handled.' He turned to Mrs. Jepson with a half-smile, 'Nevertheless, I think you may be confident the outcome will be successful.'

'Oh, I hope so — I can't tell you how worried I've been.'

'I can well imagine,' he murmured, mesmerically propelling the woman to the door. 'We shall encounter you at the séance, shall we not?'

When she had gone Doctor Morelle turned to Miss Frayle, a rather preoccupied look in his narrowed gaze.

'Kindly procure me my hat and gloves,' he bade. 'I am going to partake of a walk before luncheon. Kindly also hand me the copy of the current scurrilous journal which I perceive half concealed on your desk.'

'You've no right to confiscate it,' she protested. 'I haven't finished reading it yet.'

'Come, Miss Frayle, don't quibble. Hand it me,' he insisted testily. 'Thank you. I will scrutinise this journal with avid interest during my walk.' He gave a half-derisive smile at her expression of complete wonderment as he strode out of the study.

Miss Frayle closed her gaping mouth, and began to tidy her desk unnecessarily, and mentally counted the number of hours until the séance. This case appealed to her more than any other the Doctor had undertaken. She was, convinced in her own mind that Captain Zolta was genuinely clairvoyant. How could the Doctor then discredit him? Was this going to be a solitary occasion when he would have to retire defeated?

*　*　*

Shortly before three o'clock she and Doctor Morelle pushed through the green

43

door, which was ajar, of a small 18th century house just off Park Lane. The hall was oppressive with luxury — with thick carpets and heavy drapery.

'Isn't it exciting,' she breathed. 'All this shaded lighting and rich, velvet hangings. And the queer-smelling incense.'

'I am somewhat relieved,' he pronounced, 'to find the atmosphere singularly stuffy and thoroughly redolent of brazen quackery.' He pushed through another door. 'This will doubtless be the room where the séance is to be held.'

A group of some thirty people were sitting in a semicircle, and Doctor Morelle perceived two vacant seats next to Mrs. Jepson and her daughter. They signalled them to join them.

'Where's Captain Zolta?' whispered Miss Frayle tensely

'He doesn't appear until the exact second the séance is due to begin,' Hilary Jepson informed her. 'He'll come through those curtains just over there.'

Miss Frayle followed the gaze of everyone in the room to a pair of black curtains, embroidered with cabalistic signs, which hung down from a parabola.

She held her breath as a gong eerily sounded three strokes. Noiselessly the curtains were drawn back by unseen hands, and Captain Zolta strode into the room. He was suitably handsome and mystical-looking. A turban entwined his head, but the remainder of his garb was European and conventional. He was tall, well-knit and slim, and so far as Miss Frayle could judge would be a well-preserved fifty.

Silently he mounted a dais in the middle of the circle. Wearily, as though he was preparing for some exhausting task, he pressed a clenched hand to his forehead. The silence became electric. A woman coughed apologetically, Slowly Captain Zolta raised his head and gazed into space.

'Now, my fear friends, I am ready to draw back the veil from the future.' His voice was suave, and there was a trace of slight foreign accent. 'For your guidance, so that you may tread the path of good fortune and happiness, I will look into my crystal and speak its mind. Its mind of what is to come.'

He removed a black velvet cloth, which covered a large crystal on a wrought-iron stand.

'Here, in this crystal globe are contained the secrets of your dreams,' the Captain continued. 'Your dreams of success, of wealth, of *love* . . . Ask of me what you wish to know, and I will answer.'

Several among his audience craned forward eagerly and fluttered their hands to draw his attention.

The Captain waved a silencing arm. 'A moment! Music must play and induce that mood by which I may gaze upon the clear pages of the future and discern the hidden writing'

Music from a concealed radio-gramophone stole into the room, Doctor Morelle recognised the piece as an excerpt from a well-known classic, but Miss Frayle merely categorised it as 'creepy music'.

'Ooh, Doctor!' she gasped. 'It's very exciting!'

The music rose to a crescendo in a minor key and then faded down. Captain Zolta bowed his turbaned head to the crystal.

'Now, who first desires to know their fate?' the Captain asked in hollow tones.

Doctor Morelle craned forward and lifted his arm high, so that his request was more evident than those of the rather flurried women about him, 'Captain Zolta . . . ' he hailed imperatively.

The Captain slightly inclined his head. 'Speak, my friend what do you wish to know?'

The Doctor gazed at the tapestry-covered walls behind the clairvoyant. In carefully measured words that gave no clue to his scepticism, he said:

'There is, at this moment, Captain Zolta, a certain competition about to take place of which I would like to know the result.'

The Captain nodded. 'Yes, my friend?' he prompted.

'The competition is in the shape of a race between a number of equine beasts for monetary reward,' continued the Doctor. 'If I may descend to the vernacular for the sake of clarity, it is, in fact, known as a horse race. The race of which I speak is known as 'The Oaks', and competing in it is an animal — er

— named 'Pay Up'. It won a contest last year known as the 'Two Thousand Guineas'. Will this horse accomplish a similar feat this afternoon?'

Miss Frayle had been watching the Doctor open-mouthed as he led up to the question.

'Fancy you knowing anything about horse racing,' she whispered, 'Ssh!' hissed the Doctor, closely watching the clairvoyant who was looking into his crystal with concentrated zeal.

The Captain looked up. Softly he asked:

'Are you able my friend, to describe this horse to me so that I may distinguish it from the other competitors?'

The Doctor nodded in pretence of being helpful.

'The animal carries upon its back, for the purpose of guidance and encouragement, a young man wearing a shirt luridly coloured in purple and orange hoops, with a cap of sky blue. The quadruped also carries the number Ten. The contest in which it is engaged is due to commence at this moment.'

The clairvoyant gazed into the crystal.

'Very well,' he said softly. 'I will endeavour to picture the scene . . . ' He paused, and imperceptibly the music crept into the room again. An inspired radiance came over the Captain's face. 'Here it is,' he exclaimed. 'I can see the crowd thronging the racecourse . . . Excited, all faces are turned to where a group of horses are being marshalled at the starting place. Let me see . . . Let me see . . . Yes! There is a horse bearing a rider in purple with orange hoops, sky blue cap and the number is Ten . . . '

Miss Frayle almost fell from her chair in excitement. It was all so pictorially vivid. She felt she could almost see it herself as though on a film.

The captain resumed apparently with increasing confidence as he felt the warmth of the audience's awed admiration.

'I now see a spectator reading a card showing the names of the horses . . . I can see the name against the horse number Ten. It is 'Pay Up'. Now the crowd shouts! The horses leap forward — the race has begun. Number Ten is in the middle of the rushing animals. He is trying to break through — !'

The Captain stopped as he gazed more closely at the crystal. His lips moved spasmodically but no sound came. Agitatedly he clawed at the air. Miss Frayle glanced round to see the reaction of other people to this strange behaviour.

She saw that Hilary Jepson was actually weeping! The girl's head was held high in a proud manner, and she was making no effort to check the tears that rolled down her cheeks.

'I — I cannot — continue — I' gasped the Captain theatrically.

An excited and shocked murmur broke through the room. Hilary Jepson raced from the circle and ran to the door.

'He's ill!' gasped Miss Frayle urgently. 'Doctor! Do something!'

The clairvoyant strove to regain his breath, as the Doctor watched him dispassionately.

'I feel faint!' gasped the Captain. 'The room's so hot — so — '

Doctor Morelle languidly rose to his feet, and strode across the half circle to the dais. He chuckled sardonically as he stared down at the Captain, and challenged: 'You are sure, Captain Zolta, your fainting attack is not the result of an over-heated imagination rather than the humidity of the room?'

Captain Zolta struggled to his feet. 'What do you mean?' he shouted 'What are you saying?'

'Merely that you have precipitated yourself into the trap I prepared for you!' There was an excited hubbub in the room.

'Doctor Morelle! What trap?' insisted Miss Frayle. 'I don't understand.'

The Doctor addressed the shocked faces that were turned to him.

'Captain Zolta proves himself to be nothing more than a trickster and a charlatan!' he declared. 'Already his fiancée has become cognisant of the fact — judging from the flow from her lachrymal glands as she was departing!'

'She was weeping! I saw her,' put in Miss Frayle excitedly.

'Precisely!' He moved to the door. 'Come, Miss Frayle. Come Mrs. Jepson, you have nothing to fear now. Your daughter is quite out of the power of this impostor.'

★　★　★

Later that evening, Miss Frayle button-holed Doctor Morelle in his study.

'I can't understand exactly how you and Miss Jepson *knew* so definitely that Captain Zolta had proved himself to be a fake,' she puzzled.

'Both Miss Jepson and myself happened to be cognisant with horse racing,' he answered levelly.

'You, Doctor!'

'Yes I! And since, at my suggestion, several representatives of the press were at Captain Zolta's demonstration, his exposure was complete and final.' The Doctor gazed attentively at the tip of his Le Sphinx. 'Captain Zolta knew, of course, that he could not predict the winning horse — hence his simulated 'illness' — but he committed the ridiculous mistake of describing something which could not possibly have happened: a colt to have won the Two Thousand Guineas horse race, which is for three-year-olds, and run the following year in The Oaks, which is also for three-year-old competitors!'

Bright understanding spread over Miss Frayle's features.

'And when I think, Doctor,' she said with a laugh, 'of the way you criticised me for reading the popular press! How did you learn all about horseracing? From your scientific and medical journals?'

He regarded her icily.

'I obtained my information, Miss Frayle, through your scurrilous newspaper and through the perusal of a handbook dealing with the subject.'

She burst into uncontrollable laughter.

'I do wish I'd seen you!' she exclaimed warmly. 'It would have been wonderful to have watched your face while you studied 'form'.'

He exhaled a cloud of blue smoke.

'I took the precaution to deprive you of that doubtful pleasure by absorbing the volume's contents surreptitiously during my walk.' His voice took on a severe tone: 'Really, Miss Frayle, I must deplore your picking up such jargon as 'studying form'!'

'Oh, I know more than that,' she flashed proudly. 'For instance, I've just thought of another mistake the Captain made.'

'Indeed!' Doctor Morelle lifted his eyebrows. 'Would you care to enlighten me?'

'Well, you see, Doctor,' Miss Frayle began, 'another mistake Captain Zolta made was that 'Pay-Up' was a colt, and colts don't run in The Oaks. It's a race for girl-horses — er — follies they call them.'

'Fillies, my *dear* Miss Frayle!' corrected the Doctor impatiently. 'Not follies!'

'That's it! Fillies.' She gave a gurgling laugh. 'I knew it was something to do with a word that was foolish or silly!'

'Enough of this futile badinage. I am apt to find your gaiety a trifle exhausting. I think perhaps a little dictation may have a normalising effect on you. Will you kindly read me the notes I dictated this morning?'

Miss Frayle sighed as she turned back the pages of her notebook. She studied the hieroglyphics and began to re-quote:

' "The happenings in a single day often form a loosely related — and even completely disjointed — procession of incidents. Invariably these incidents present an apparently insoluble problem, be it sociological or criminal. By collating the facts as they present themselves to an intelligent observer, the complete solution to that problem will be apparent. Paragraph'.'

She broke off and gazed at him with thoughtful innocence. 'You know, Doctor, that sounds wonderful, but I'm sure it's one of those theories which don't work out in practice. You see, I believe — ' She paused to marshal her thoughts.

'Proceed, Miss Frayle,' Doctor Morelle said coldly. 'I await, with confidence, that you are about to make some pronouncement which will revolutionise the entire field of metaphysics and psycho-pathology!'

'Well, take today, for instance.' She tapped the pencil against her teeth. 'Something happened this morning that wasn't related in any way with the happenings of the rest of the day — '

'I should have imagined that you would

have been more tactful if you had not mentioned your carelessness in allowing that young medical student to gain entrance to my study under the pretence of being a plumber! If that is to what you are referring.'

'Yes, Doctor. Now Mr. Page presented a problem,' she hazarded, 'and he appeared to be a deserving young man. Yet his problem's unsolved, and so is that of Miss Hilary Jepson up to a point.'

'So I am to assume that my whole day's labour has been useless,' he murmured with a derisive smile.

'Oh, no, Doctor — you saved Miss Jepson from the clutches of that fake clairvoyant, but in doing so you made her heartbroken. Of course it wasn't your fault,' conceded Miss Frayle, 'but at the same time it just shows that problems aren't so completely solved as your theory states they are.'

He walked to her desk with measured steps.

'Before we proceed any further, Miss Frayle, would you retrieve from the wastepaper basket those two theatre tickets which an over-optimistic theatrical manager dispatched to me in the afternoon post, and would you forward them to the young man?' he asked coldly.

'But how's that going to help him?' she queried.

'Also enclose a note with Miss Jepson's address and suggest he makes her acquaintance and invite her to the theatre, informing him that I leave the case entirely in his hands! Now are you satisfied, Miss Frayle?'

She smiled understandingly, and broke into a girlish laugh.

'I see, Doctor! Oh, it would be funny to see you with little wings indulging in archery!'

'Little wings! Archery!' he echoed sternly. 'What nonsense are you uttering now?'

'I was referring to — ' Her eyes danced impishly behind her spectacles — 'to — Cupid!'

He nodded weightily. 'Ah, assuredly — the classical, allegorical personification of the uninhibited expression of the libido — popularly known as Love.'

'Precisely, Doctor Morelle!'

3

THE CASE OF THE
FLOATING HERMIT

They caught the 6.22 from Waterloo to
Parkham Creek, and found, as the train
steamed out, they had the compartment
to themselves. Miss Frayle sat in a corner
seat and watched the suburbs of Greater
London slip past. The streets, blocks of
flats and factories were bathed in a golden
haze of fading evening sunlight, lending
to their begrimed, unprepossessing exteri-
ors a fleeting appearance of brightness
and glowing colour.

Presently, her eyes a little dazzled by
the shining vista slipping swiftly past,
Miss Frayle blinked and turned from the
window. She adjusted her spectacles,
picked up the evening paper and then
paused to bestow a glance at Doctor
Morelle opposite her. He was reading a
book with what appeared to be avid

interest. She was about to look at her paper when she caught the title of the book and the author's name, and she gave a little sigh.

He did not raise his eyes from the page, but, tapping the ash off his cigarette, observed: 'Finding the journey tedious already, my dear Miss Frayle?'

She started, and laughed with a little embarrassment. 'Why, what made you think that, Doctor?'

'I was under the impression you had given a yawn of ennui.'

'No. I — er — just sighed, that's all.'

'In a somewhat melancholy mood, perhaps?'

He continued reading and she wriggled with annoyance. Why did he always pounce on her with a question to which she could give no ready answer? 'I didn't know I had sighed, as a matter of fact — ' she began, then bit her lip as she realised she had only a moment before admitted she had.

'To prevaricate successfully, a retentive memory is essential,' he murmured. 'And yours would seem to be woefully short!'

He flashed her a glance, narrow-eyed and searching. 'However, if you have some secret which you prefer to withhold from me, I have, of course, no desire to drag it from you.' He compressed his lips and returned to his book.

Oh, dear! groaned Miss Frayle inwardly. She had looked forward to the journey all day, and it had only just begun and she had unwittingly annoyed him. She fiddled with her spectacles, looked out of the window again and then stared at her newspaper unseeingly. If only she could have thought of something to say! Not the truth, of course, that would have made him more sardonically irritable than her silly little lie. No, she couldn't reveal her sigh had been actuated by the fact the book he was reading was one he had written himself. She couldn't admit she had sighed with wonder at the blatant conceit that had prompted him to bring the book with him in the hope other passengers would notice it and the name of its author! It was a large volume, conspicuously bound. And there he was, pretending to be absorbed in it as if he was reading it for the first time.

He raised his head suddenly and, through a cloud of cigarette smoke, said: 'I hope you do not imagine I have brought this volume with me for any ulterior motive? I think I may say I am not quite so vainglorious as to wish to flaunt my works before the public at large!'

She could only goggle at him in stupid amazement. It was moments like these when she felt convinced he was not human, but possessed of some extraordinary power which she hazily associated with Cagliostro, voodooism, high priests of the occult and the ability to see through a woman. For this was when she was certain he could read her innermost thoughts, could see into the limitless future. This was Doctor Morelle at his most frightening!

The train roared into a tunnel. The compartment was plunged into inky blackness before the electric lights tardily came on, and when she looked next at him his saturnine face was bent once more over his book. She might have imagined he was as deeply engrossed in its pages as before — but for the sardonic smile that she could discern flickering at the corners of his mouth.

Doctor Morelle had accepted an invitation to spend the weekend at the country house of Henry Myers, the founder of the famous firm of manufacturing chemists. A Northerner of the self-made industrial type, he was also a man intensely interested in scientific research. He had contributed a large part of his fortune for the furtherance of work in this sphere. He had chanced to hear one of the Doctor's lectures on a particular aspect of biochemistry relating to industrial workers and had introduced himself. The Doctor had been favourably impressed by his good-humoured, simple and straightforward personality; and, incidentally, flattered not a little by the man's respectful thirst for knowledge on scientific subjects. Hence the acceptance of Myers invitation to visit him. Miss Frayle had also been included in the invitation.

The train was now running through open country. Miss Frayle, who had been glancing idly through her paper, looked up with a sudden exclamation: 'Parkham Creek? Isn't that where we're going, Doctor?'

'To the best of my knowledge, yes. Have you any reason — apart from idle curiosity — for asking?'

She indicated an item in the newspaper with some excitement. 'In tonight's paper! It says — '

'Do you feel that what, as you so vaguely put it, 'it says', can be of sufficient interest to me that I should interrupt reading my book?'

She stammered under the rebuke. 'I — I thought you might like to see. It's this paragraph here.' She read aloud:

' 'Mysterious Hermit Drowned. Body Not Yet Recovered . . . Early this morning,' Miss Frayle went on, ' 'the body of a man was seen by two farm labourers being carried out to sea. The men hurried to the beach and a fisherman took them out in a rowing boat in the hope of overtaking the body. By that time, however, it had disappeared from sight and the men failed to locate it. Returning to shore they informed the police, and subsequent inquiries revealed that a local character known as Old Charlie the Hermit was missing from the hut where he lived. It is believed it is his body that was seen floating out to sea . . . ''

Miss Frayle paused for breath. Doctor Morelle said: 'Most interesting. Most interesting! And now, I hope, my dear Miss Frayle, I may be permitted to return to my book? Thank you!'

'But didn't you hear?' she squeaked, 'it was at Parkham Creek!'

He looked up sharply. 'Why, we are proceeding there! Why did you not mention that fact before?'

She ignored his unjust accusation. She rushed on, unable to resist an anticipated moment of triumph. 'And if you'd let me finish reading,' she said, 'I would have told you that the two farm labourers are employed by Mr. Myers.'

'Perhaps if you would be good enough to hand me the journal so that I may peruse it myself . . . ? Thank you . . . Now I may at last obtain a coherent account of the incident to which you have mumblingly referred!' He read the account quickly and returned the paper to her without any comment. He picked up his book and it was not until some moments later that he murmured, half to himself: 'One would imagine it to be a case of *felo-de-se*. People who pursue a solitary existence tend to abnormalities of thought and behaviour.' And he puffed at his cigarette as if to dismiss the matter as one of little importance.

Some time later the train drew into a typical branch line station, and a porter was calling out in a country burr: 'Parkham Creek! Parkham Creek Station . . . ' Doctor Morelle and Miss Frayle alighted and dumped their suitcases on the platform. Miss Frayle sniffed the fresh, sea-laden air.

'Ooh! What lovely air! I'm going to enjoy this weekend!'

'It seems we might expect somewhat recalcitrant weather,' the Doctor said, eyeing a distant mass of dark, heavy cloud. But even he could not dampen her sudden wave of high spirits, and she laughed irrepressibly. He contemplated her with raised eyebrows and a somewhat disagreeable expression but said nothing. A man in a chauffeur's uniform approached them and touched his cap.

'Doctor Morelle? Miss Frayle — ?'

'Good evening,' she smiled at him.

He grinned back. ' 'Evening, miss, Good evening, sir. I'm from Mr. Myers,' he said in a pleasant sounding burr. He stood there a little indecisive and the Doctor indicated the suitcases.

'Would you take them?' he said sharply.

The man started and picked them up. 'Sorry sir! I — I was wandering a bit.' He marched off sturdily towards the station exit. They followed, giving up their ticket-halves to the friendly porter-cum-ticket-collector-cum-stationmaster, who wished them a cheery 'Goodnight.' The chauffeur had the car door open for them and was stacking the suitcases into the seat beside him.

As Doctor Morelle followed Miss Frayle into the car the man said: 'This suicide has upset us a bit round here and

I wasn't thinking properly.' He was evidently explaining his absent-mindedness on the platform. The Doctor lit a Le Sphinx, and glanced at the lowering sky. 'The inclement weather I prophesied should make itself felt unpleasantly soon!' he murmured.

'Aye,' agreed the chauffeur, cocking an eye out of the window and starting the car. As they drove off, Miss Frayle was wearing a preoccupied frown. 'Poor man,' she said, half to herself, 'how awful, committing suicide.' The man in front darted a quick look back at her. He had caught her words referring to his explanatory remarks — the window separating the driving seat from the back of the car was down — and he nodded with a lower lip glumly protruding. 'Ah . . .' he said, and gave his attention to the road again.

Doctor Morelle blew out a cloud of cigarette smoke. 'Has it been established it is a case of *felo-de-se*?'

'Beg pardon, sir?' said the chauffeur over his shoulder.

'Self-inflicted homicide.'

The man still didn't get it. 'Ah — er

— that is — ah, er — ' he mumbled.

'Doctor Morelle means is it certain the poor man took his own life?' Miss Frayle explained.

'Thank you, Miss Frayle!' said the Doctor mockingly.

'Oh . . . ' said the chauffeur. 'Oh, yes, he didn't fall into the Creek accidental — But you seem to know a bit about it yourselves.'

'It was in tonight's paper.'

'Was it, Miss? Well now . . . ' He clicked his teeth and shook his head in wonderment. 'The news don't half get round quick — especially if it's bad news!'

Miss Frayle laughed. The other went on: 'No, Old Charlie was too careful for it to've bin an accident. And he hadn't got no enemies — hardly spoke to anyone — so nobody did it purposely, nor nothing like that.'

'Do they know why he committed suicide?'

The chauffeur shook his head.

'They do say he had a tidy bit o' cash stowed away,' he volunteered, 'so it couldn't have been money trouble.'

They rounded a bend and came in sight of an estuary flowing swiftly seawards and dominated on either side by ragged cliffs.

'That's Old Charlie's hut, across the field yonder,' said the chauffeur, indicating a small, derelict-looking bungalow with a single chimney. It had a deserted and solitary appearance in the fading light. A stile and a narrow footpath marked the approach to it.

'You might pull up for a moment,' said Doctor Morelle, and the car was brought obediently to a standstill near the stile.

'I was afraid of this!' sighed Miss Frayle.

The Doctor paid no attention to her remark, if indeed he heard it; he sat thoughtfully contemplating the landscape.

'Isn't it getting rather dark to go for a walk?' she went on insinuatingly.

'You are anticipating my thoughts, Miss Frayle,' he said.

'Oh,' she said in a tone of relief, misunderstanding his response, 'I thought you were going to have a look at the hermit's hut.'

'That is precisely what I propose to do!' he murmured. And he quickly opened the door and got out. 'If you are in the least apprehensive, however, by all means remain in the car. The chauffeur and I will not be long, I feel certain.'

'I — I think I'd rather come with you,' she hurriedly decided. She was not particularly enamoured with the prospect of remaining alone on the deserted road in the gathering dusk.

'If you will lead the way,' Doctor Morelle murmured to the chauffeur.

The man first extracted a torch from one of the side pockets of the car. Presently they stood at the door of the hut. The door was unlocked. As Doctor Morelle pushed it open and entered, there was a slight sound of scuffling from a corner. Miss Frayle, following close behind drew back with a startled cry.

'Oh! What's that?'

'Calm yourself,' chuckled the Doctor mirthlessly. 'They are merely small rodents of the genus Mus.'

'Mice!' gasped Miss Frayle, horrified. She rushed to jump on an old chair that stood by the table.

'S'orl right, Miss,' the chauffeur reassured her. 'They've 'opped it.'

'I wonder what attracted them,' pondered the Doctor, looking round the room. His gaze fell upon a table in the centre of the room. As he approached it he observed a small piece of cheese on a plate, beside which was a knife and other obvious indications of a meal. The cheese was almost entirely covered with mildew.

'Ah yes, the deceased's last meal which, if you will have the courage to approach more closely, might be worthy of inspection.' Miss Frayle followed him to the table. 'Observe the minute fungi known as mildew, Miss Frayle. One might almost describe it as fur-coated, so heavy is the fungus!' No one smiled at his somewhat heavy attempt at humour. He sighed. 'Never mind! Let us return to the car.'

'I'm sure Mr. Myers will be wondering what's happened to us,' said Miss Frayle, welcoming the opportunity to leave the desolate hut.

'He may possibly be interested in my explanation of our delay,' said Doctor Morelle, as they made their way back to the road.

Shortly afterwards — just before a heavy downpour of rain began — they had reached their destination, and their host was conducting them into a comfortable lounge hall, where a huge log fire blazed cheerily. Miss Frayle began to feel her drooping spirits revive.

'Yes . . . I was beginning to think ye'd missed train or something,' said Myers in a marked Yorkshire burr.

'I fear it was sheer inquisitiveness on my part which is responsible for our belated arrival,' admitted Doctor Morelle.

'I was afraid you'd think we'd got lost,' Miss Frayle smiled.

'Well, you've got here and that's the main thing — and before you got caught in the storm!' and the other handed a sherry to Miss Frayle. He observed to Doctor Morelle: 'They say every real scientist is inquisitive. I'm a bit of a busybody myself.' And he chuckled good-naturedly.

'I paused en route to investigate the mystery of the hermit's murder.'

'Murder?' repeated Miss Frayle in a startled tone, goggling at the Doctor, who seemed blandly unconscious of the significance of his remark.

'Murder!' laughed Myers. 'You mean suicide . . . Poor Old Charlie — It was two of my men spotted his body floating on the tide. They rushed and got a boat to try and get him, but he must have gone well out to sea — they couldn't find any trace of him. The police have been up here checking their story, I know.'

'The body has not so far been recovered?'

'No, but it was him all right. The men recognised his long hair and beard he wore — eccentric old boy he was. And anyway he's disappeared from his hut.'

They heard the front doorbell ring.

'That'll be Harvey, my agent,' explained Myers. 'He'll tell you all about the suicide, Doctor. I believe he was the last to see the old chap alive.'

Harvey proved to be a man in the middle thirties, with dark eyes and a genial, brisk manner. He laid what appeared to be a number of business papers and account books on a side table. Myers introduced him to his guests.

'The Doctor seems to have an idea that old Charlie was murdered — wasn't suicide,' he said as he poured the newcomer a drink.

Harvey laughed easily.

'Oh yes? The police would be glad to know about that I'm sure,' he chuckled, taking the glass the other handed him. He went on confidently: 'They happen to have discovered exactly how the whole accident occurred.'

Myers looked at him sharply.

'Accident?' he queried. 'But I thought it was — '

'I'm afraid we were all wrong, Mr. Myers,' the agent confessed.

'That makes the — ah — incident even more intriguing,' declared Doctor Morelle, lighting one of his inevitable cigarettes.

'Well, let's hear the latest news about it, anyway,' Myers said.

Harvey glanced at them. His manner suggested that he was inclined to enjoy occupying the centre of attention.

'Well . . . ' he began, taking a drink. 'It was I who saw the old chap this morning — about five o'clock. I was getting up, and happened to catch sight of him through my bedroom window. He was making for the wooden bridge over the narrow part of the creek — coming from the direction of Long Oak field where he has his hut.'

'Did you see him actually in transit over the bridge?' asked the Doctor.

The man shook his head.

'I wish I had,' he said regretfully, 'because I might have saved him. But I just called out to him through my open window, and he waved back. Then I went straight down to breakfast.'

Myers said: 'Go on . . . '

'It seems the bridge-rail must have been rotten in the middle, and as old Charlie leaned on it, it must have snapped — '

'Why should he lean on the rail as heavily as all that?' murmured Doctor Morelle shrewdly. 'Surely a handrail would be a light affair — merely a precautionary safeguard?'

Myers shot the Doctor a look appreciative of a point he had raised.

'I've seen Old Charlie lean on that rail many a time,' Harvey explained readily. 'He used to rest there for a few minutes and look down into the water. You know how people do when they stand on a bridge.'

'Yes, that's true enough,' conceded Myers.

'Yes, I like to myself,' said Miss Frayle. 'So long as it doesn't make me feel giddy!'

'The police examined the rail a little while ago,' the other went on. 'It was pretty rotten.'

The Doctor looked at his host.

'What time did your men see the body floating out to sea?'

'Er — seven o'clock, that was.'

'That's right,' nodded Harvey. 'The police say two hours is about the time it would take from the bridge to reach the point where your men saw it, the tide running as it does.'

The Doctor carefully examined the tip

of his Le Sphinx.

'How extremely fortuitous,' he observed in a silk-like tone, 'that the tide should be on the turn when the — ah — accident occurred!'

'How d'you mean, Doctor?' It was Myers who asked the question.

Doctor Morelle smiled frostily. In a manner suggesting he was explaining an obviously simple fact, he murmured: 'Merely that had the rail collapsed when the tide was coming in, the corpse would have been washed ashore to provide evidence.'

Harvey's face widened in an expansive grin of toleration.

'You still seem pretty sure it was murder, Doctor Morelle!'

'The term 'pretty sure' is in this case an understatement!' He paused melodramatically, and Miss Frayle goggled at him through her spectacles as he said quietly: 'I can place my hands on the murderer now . . . '

'Well, well,' said Myers in an indulgent tone. 'I'm sure we'd like to hear more of your theories, Doctor.'

Harvey nodded genially, although there was a sting behind his words as he said:

'Yes . . . We don't always get the chance to hear an expert's views on this sort of thing . . . '

Doctor Morelle merely smiled thinly through a puff of cigarette smoke.

'I doubt if this is quite the correct moment to make any such disclosures,' he said with a judicious air. 'But I will give one or two indications as to why the suicide theory is obviously in error. First of all, on visiting the deceased's hut, I discovered a piece of cheese somewhat heavily mildewed on the table. This was incompatible with the suggestion it had formed part of a meal of which he had partaken this morning. That mildew would have taken more than one day to form.'

'H'm, something in that,' said Myers.

'Yes,' conceded the other man. 'But hardly conclusive evidence, though. You mean it indicates that he was killed some days ago?'

Doctor Morelle nodded. He said: 'Furthermore, the body of a drowned human being does not rise to the surface for several days.' He glanced at Myers. 'Yet your employees witnessed it floating out to sea this morning.'

Myers appeared obviously impressed.

'You're right there,' he said slowly. He turned towards Harvey about to say something and stopped short. The agent's face was contorted with murderous fury.

'Don't move — any of you — don't move — !'

Miss Frayle gave a sharp gasping scream as a black automatic pistol appeared in his hand. His eyes darted from one face to another, as he weighed up his chance of escape.

There came a sudden ring at the front door. Doctor Morelle, who had remained unmoved by Harvey's reaction to his words, now glanced at his host. With an elaborately simulated apology in his voice, he murmured:

'I fear I forgot to mention the fact that on my way here I paused at the telephone-box at the crossroads to request the local police authorities to visit me at their earliest convenience. That will, no doubt, be them.'

Harvey stared at the Doctor like a trapped animal. Hs took two rapid steps backwards towards the door, his gun still menacing them, and then suddenly appeared to stumble. Before he could regain his balance, Myers had thrown himself at him. Doctor Morelle promptly gained possession of the revolver as it was jerked out of the man's grasp. Harvey's resistance collapsed as Miss Frayle rushed to admit the local police-sergeant and a constable.

★ ★ ★

Later the Doctor addressed Miss Frayle in a censorious tone:

'I really must reprimand you about the habit of sprawling your feet halfway across the room!'

'But, Doctor Morelle — ' she protested, 'I tripped him up deliberately!'

He permitted himself a thin smile of scepticism. 'Were you not too occupied in drawing a deep breath preparatory to screaming for help?' he retorted.

She ignored the remark to ask:

'Did — did he confess?'

'Certainly. He bludgeoned the old man to death some days ago.'

'But why?'

'He had embezzled a sum of Myers' money, and was anxious to replace it before the yearly audit. As it transpired, his crime was fruitless, for his victim had, in fact, no secret hoard whatever.'

'Did he break the bridge handrail?'

He nodded: 'Harvey broke it deliberately in order to lend colour to his entirely fabricated story.'

'Well,' said Miss Frayle, 'I must say if I were going to murder anybody for their money, I should jolly well make sure it was there first!'

Doctor Morelle clicked his tongue in mock disapproval.

'Tck! Tck! Can this cold and calculating tone be that of my prim and meek Miss Frayle!' He went on, his saturnine face bent close to hers: 'Have you, by any chance, made certain of the whereabouts of my secret hoard of gold?'

She smiled at him disarmingly.

'Oh, I should never dream of murdering you, Doctor Morelle!'

He eyed her narrowly,

'Thank you! I'm deeply touched,' he said. Then, with deepening suspicion, 'Is there any particular reason for this charitable feeling you harbour towards me?'

She regarded him blandly from behind her spectacles.

'Only that you'd be bound to pop up afterwards to jeer at me and point out the incriminating mistake I'd made!' she said.

4

THE CASE OF THE CLEVER DOG

Doctor Morelle had been visiting a patient who was resident in a luxurious hotel near Piccadilly, while Miss Frayle sat in a corner of the lounge, watching the pageant of metropolitan hotel life. She found it all rather fun to 'study types' as she called it, deciding that the party by the reception desk were Americans; that the smartly-dressed gentleman choosing a cigar ostentatiously was really a confidence trickster. Celebrities strolling to the grillroom gave her a thrill. She was rather sorry, therefore, when the Doctor appeared from the lift after only half an hour, and her idle speculations were interrupted.

'I've had such an interesting time, watching people,' she told him. 'A big hotel is really a most fascinating place — '

The Doctor was in no mood, however, to listen to her obvious opinions.

'This hotel is the cretin's dream of Babylon,' he declared, snubbing her. 'I find the sybarite atmosphere definitely oppressive. Come, Miss Frayle, we will walk back to Harley Street since we have no further appointments.'

She followed him into Piccadilly. They plunged through the narrow streets, across Shaftesbury Avenue towards cosmopolitan Soho. Here, the contrast between luxury and everyday squalor was marked. Foreign languages were being spoken all around them. From the cafés and restaurants wafted a smell of greasy food. People jostled against them — some of them sinister-looking, with queer clothes and shifty eyes.

As they went deeper into the heart of Soho, it seemed as though they were in a foreign land. Sounds and voices combined to make a curious medley. Street buskers were playing mouth organs, accordions, and one man was strumming at a piano on wheels. Miss Frayle kept near to the Doctor — this romanticised district was compellingly fascinating and yet definitely frightening to her. She would never have dared to come here alone.

They had to pause at a street intersection, and she noticed a seedy-looking individual with a walking stick and a dog, who stood in the gutter a few yards along from a hairdressing saloon. His back being turned towards her, she hadn't been able to help noticing that the man's hair hung in a ragged fringe over the collar of his shabby overcoat.

'Oh, look at that poor man!' she sympathised. 'Doesn't he look the picture of misery?'

'Hm! Manic depressive type,' the Doctor diagnosed. 'Or, more probably, a professional mendicant.'

'He may be a deserving case, you never know,' Miss Frayle said thoughtfully, and with a mixture of good nature towards the beggar and defiance to the Doctor, she extracted some coppers from her hand-bag, and walked in the roadway towards the beggar.

Doctor Morelle watched her silently as

she spoke kindly to the forlorn figure, and she patted the dog's head. He noticed, too, that the man wore dark glasses, and on the tray containing bootlaces that he carried was pinned a notice indicating that he was blind. As the man took her coins, the Doctor noted, with his uncanny gift for detail, that the top of the man's right thumb was missing.

And then, in turning from his contemplation of the figures of the man and the dog, and Miss Frayle acting the Lady Bountiful, he caught sight of himself in the mirror by a café door. It was an old mirror, spotty and cracked, but it sufficed to show him that while his case wasn't so bad as that of the man over the way, still it was about time he paid a visit to the barber's chair.

His wandering eyes then alighted on a barber's pole almost opposite, and immediately he made the decision.

'I am reminded, Miss Frayle, that I am in need of tonsorial attention myself,' he declared as she returned to his side.

'Yes, Doctor. I'll telephone Trumpers this afternoon for an appointment.'

'That will not be necessary. Fortuitously there is an establishment in this vicinity.'

'But you can't go in there,' she protested. 'They wouldn't give you a good hair cut.'

'I do not happen to be addicted to vanity. This establishment will well suit my purpose,' he snapped impulsively. 'And you will be able to imbibe a cup of tea in the opposite café while you are waiting.'

As he finished his sentence he strode into the barber's shop. Miss Frayle entered the dark café, and sat down at a dirty, marble-topped table, while other customers eyed her suspiciously. She moved near to the window so that she would be able to see the Doctor immediately he left the shop.

Meanwhile the hairdressing saloon, Doctor Morelle discovered, held three chairs, two of which were occupied, and as there were no other customers waiting, he took his place straight away in the remaining chair.

'A hair cut. And kindly refrain from

amputating my ears!'

'Right you are, sir!'

The young fellow grinned and set to work. He was used to all sorts of queer customers, and this bloke looked a proper gent and might cough up a good tip. Doctor Morelle looked up for a moment at the entrance of a man who, after a genial response to greetings from each of the barbers, sat down patiently to wait.

He deduced that the newcomer was a regular customer, for he was assured it would not be long before he would be attended to. Showily the man produced a thin, black cigar and lit it. His features were long and sallow and there was a curious, twisted little smile that seemed continually to play about the corners of his mouth,

Doctor Morelle, though only obliquely interested in the judgment of character through physiognomy, had already come to the conclusion that it was a sadistic, rapacious mouth, when the man picked up a newspaper and began to read.

Presently the Doctor's narrowed eyes watched the door again as another man came in. This second man looked at the occupied chairs and, after being informed there would soon be one vacant for him, he sat next to the man with the cigar. After a quick almost ferrety glance at him, the latter went on reading. The newcomer seemed to be a stranger to the establishment, and through the mirror Doctor Morelle bent a speculative gaze upon him. He eyed him as, putting his hands in his pockets, he leaned back lowering his eyelids as if thinking deeply. He observed the hard line of his jaw. In spite of his almost somnolent attitude there was a watchfulness about him, a tenseness, it seemed, that was faintly evil.

Although the Doctor had come in when the other customers were already occupying chairs, his requirements had turned out to be less than theirs — he had firmly eschewed having his head singed or shampooed or anything else done to it — and so he was ready before either of them. The voluminous garment that had enveloped him and was now covered with scattered bits of his hair was removed, and he rubbed his face and down the back of his collar with a towel handed to him.

He was interrupted by a sudden exclamation from the young man who was attending him, and he looked up in time to see the customer with the black cigar crumple in his seat and pitch forward upon his face.

There were some moments of confusion, when the man who had been sitting next to the other took command of the situation.

'Let me look at him,' the man said. 'I'm a doctor.'

Doctor Morelle shot a quick look at this individual but oddly enough refrained from stating that he himself had unusual qualifications in the field of medicine. Not, of course, through modesty or even indifference to the victim's suffering, but because the Doctor's strange perception for detail had caused him to realise that something of a sinister nature was afoot. Exactly what and with what motive was not yet apparent. However, with his uncanny faculty for always taking the right course, he knew he would be best serving humanity and the cause of justice by remaining silent and watching points. He saw the man kneel down and begin to unloosen the inert figure's collar. The man then grabbed the limp arm and, with his right hand, felt the pulse. There was a tightening of his lips and he looked away.

'Get me a taxi somebody. I'll take him along to my hospital right away.'

'Is — is he — ?' someone began to ask.

'He's very ill,' was the snapped reply.

Doctor Morelle paused in the lighting of a Le Sphinx. His manner was casual enough.

'I'll procure you a taxicab,' he offered impassively, and began to go out of the door.

The other shot him a sharp look — maybe because of the Doctor's pompous tone. 'Make it snappy,' the man called after him.

Thus, Miss Frayle, from the opposite café, saw the Doctor emerge from the barber's shop, minus his hat and coat, and waving a hand while his lips formed the word: 'Taxi!' She was relieved to see him again, even though he was behaving so unconventionally. The tea that had been served to her was greasy and the cup was cracked, so that she had not dared even to sip at it. Worse still, a swarthy gigolo type had sat at her table — although there were plenty of seats elsewhere — and he had never once taken his eyes off her. She rose quickly and ran to the door.

'Hey — yer 'aven't paid!' a hoarse voice shouted after her.

'Oh — I'm so — sorry . . . I quite forgot.'

'That's all right, beautiful!' With a grand gesture the gigolo-type tossed a couple of coins on to the cracked marble, and, with a wink at the proprietor, followed her out of the café. She heard the proprietor say: 'These bilkers! It's the quiet ones that are the worst.' She blushed in humiliation. The gigolo-type was touching her arm.

'On the rocks, sister?' he queried, as though he would have been delighted if she actually had been in that precarious position. 'I might be able to — '

What plan this character might have had for Miss Frayle's future was mercifully never revealed. With a startled glance at him she fled across the road and grabbed Doctor Morelle's arm for protection.

A taxi had now drawn up outside the hairdressing saloon's open door. The man who claimed he was a doctor looked up from the unconscious figure still stretched out on the floor, and there was an anxious expression on his face,

'Going to be a mighty near thing,' he said.

Aided by one of the men of the shop, he got the limp body into the taxi. Jumping in after him, he gave the driver the name of a nearby hospital, and slammed the door. With the others, Doctor Morelle stood and watched the taxi drive off into the gathering dusk.

'What's happened, Doctor?' Miss Frayle puzzled, gazing up at him with round, wondrous eyes. 'Why didn't you help the poor man?'

'I am more likely to be of assistance by

pursuing the unobvious course,' he retorted enigmatically. He re-entered the hairdressing saloon and, after a moment, reappeared wearing his overcoat and hat and carrying his fabulous walking stick. With puzzled Miss Frayle at his side, he began walking, suddenly stopped, wheeled round on his heels and glanced up and down the street.

'Hm . . . the blind person who was hawking shoelaces does not appear to be in sight,' he observed.

'He went, Doctor Morelle.'

'When?'

'A few seconds after you'd gone for a haircut. I was watching him from the window — '

'And which direction did he take?'

'Straight ahead. He went into a doorway just up the street,' she said with a puzzled frown.

Doctor Morelle strode ahead with long raking strides. He halted after a few yards.

'Was this the doorway?'

'I think so.'

It was then they heard the whining of a dog close at hand. Doctor Morelle looked about him to locate the sound and saw he was outside the window of a ground floor flat which had a 'To Let' sign in it. And it was from here the cry seemed to be coming. The house the flat belonged to was grim-looking and shabby. Striding through the main entrance, the Doctor found a door behind which he could hear the dog whining. He grasped the handle and turned, but the door did not give. It was locked. Moving towards the head of a dark stairway farther along the hall he called down into the dim basement, from which issued a smell composite of months of boiling cabbage, kippers and fried bacon.

'Is anyone there?'

In due course a frowsy woman appeared from the basement and demanded to know his business. She was the wife of the caretaker whom, it appeared, was away ill. She eyed Doctor Morelle and Miss Frayle suspiciously as she wiped her hands on a piece of sacking which served as an apron.

'A canine appears to be trapped in the front apartment.'

'Ey?'

'He means there's a dog in there and it can't get out!' Miss Frayle translated.

'Thank you, Miss Frayle,' the Doctor acknowledged, without the least gratitude.

'T'ain't your dog is it?' the woman asked with marked hostility.

'It is not.'

'Then wot the devil are you werriting about? I've enough to do without 'aving to drag up them stairs ter be bothered by nosey parkers.'

'Kindly release the animal without delay. Unless you prefer to be reported to the Society whose duty it is to spare the suffering of such creatures.'

The woman mumbled, bit her lip and fumbled round her waist for a bunch of keys attached to a grubby length of string. She unlocked the flat door and held it open for the Doctor and Miss Frayle to enter. Across a passage came the excited yelps and scrambling of the dog from behind another door. The Doctor opened it and the animal shot out. Stepping quickly on the end of the lead which trailed after it, he prevented the overjoyed mongrel from racing excitedly out to the street. It continued to strain at the leash, while Miss Frayle, with maternal solicitude, bent down and patted it comfortingly. She became aware that the dog's appearance was familiar.

'Why, Doctor,' she exclaimed, 'it's the dog belonging to the blind man!'

'Your powers of perception are unique, my dear Miss Frayle,' he retorted with thinly veiled sarcasm.

'But why did you force your way into here?' she demanded, determined not to be crushed. 'The dog really wasn't suffering.'

'Possibly not,' he conceded. 'However I think an inspection of this apartment may be singularly revealing.'

He moved to the flat door and ascertained that the frowsy woman had returned to her subterranean domestic domain. He then returned to the room where the mongrel had been. His narrowed gaze fell upon a crowded table. He walked over to it, the dog straining behind them as Miss Frayle wrapped the leash more securely round her fingers.

The objects which had caught the Doctor's eyes included a straggly-haired wig, a pair of dark glasses, a tray containing bootlaces, a piece of cardboard with the word 'BLIND' written on it, and leaning against the table, a walking stick. Thrown over a chair nearby, which was the only other piece of furniture in the room, he saw also a shabby overcoat, an old suit and a decrepit hat.

'Well I — ' gasped Miss Frayle, her eyes behind her spectacles forming two round O's.

The Doctor gestured sweepingly. 'Observe, my dear Miss Frayle, the stock in trade of the professional mendicant.'

'You mean he wasn't really blind? And he wore a wig to make it look as though he needed a haircut? And — and he probably didn't need to wear old clothes. Is that what it means?'

'Precisely!'

'And I gave him money — the wretch!' She worked herself into a flurry of indignation. 'It's such fakes who make people too disillusioned to do good turns. Why don't you report him to the police?'

'I intend to,' he murmured, 'though not for fraudulent mendicancy.'

'What for, then?'

'That will indubitably be vouchsafed in due course,' he smiled superciliously, realising full well how tantalising it was for Miss Frayle not to be able to share the fruits of his unusual deductive talents.

'I perceived a telephone booth in the vicinity,' he resumed. 'A call to Scotland Yard would, I think, be indicated.' He tapped the ash from his Le Sphinx into the fireplace. 'Since this appears to be a straightforward case, I think I can entrust the more routine inquiries to the unsubtle — but sometimes crudely effective — methods of Detective-Inspector Hood. Come, Miss Frayle.'

'What shall I do with the dog, Doctor?'

He paused, then appeared to decide suddenly. 'Retain your grasp upon its lead,' he bade thoughtfully.

With the mongrel leaping ahead of them, they walked along the street to where the telephone was situated. The Doctor dialled Whitehall 1212 and got through immediately. 'Doctor Morelle here,' he announced. 'Please connect me with Detective-Inspector Hood.'

There followed a short pause and then:

'Hello, Doctor! Solved another murder for me?' It was Inspector Hood's genial voice.

The Doctor responded with a sardonic chuckle.

'Inevitably, I fear it will be homicide,' he responded laconically. 'The crime was in fact perpetrated in my presence — '

'Then you've got the murderer covered with your swordstick, eh, Doctor?'

'Not on this occasion. You see, although the homicide occurred in my presence I had no opportunity of preventing it occurring. True, I might have prevented the murderer from disappearing with the corpse in a taxicab, but on the other hand, it seemed a logical opportunity for leaving the scientific ratiocination and the interception of the perpetrator to Scotland Yard.'

'You — mean — mean you've deliberately let him get away?' stammered the Detective-Inspector, making explosive noises at the other end of the telephone.

'Precisely!' The Doctor was irritatingly bland. 'Since I decided that you should finish this case, gain all the credit, and further promotion would then be inevitable.'

'That's very kind of you, but what'll they do to me if I don't find the murderer — ?'

'Come, come! Surely you don't contemplate failure?'

'Not exactly. But all the same, I'd feel happier if you'd hang round to lend a hand.'

Doctor Morelle sighed resignedly, 'Very well.' His aquiline features moved closer to the mouthpiece. 'Now listen attentively while I give you all the relevant details.' He continued speaking incisively, and he finished with the words: 'It appears that the man who posed as the blind beggar and later as the doctor conveying the dead man to the hospital were one and the same person. Although the 'blind' man's disguise was clever, one detail was overlooked. Both men had the top of the right thumbs missing, proving them conclusively to be identical.'

'So it seems,' came Hood's voice 'Pretty smart of you to tumble to it. I'll be down there as quickly as I can. Where is the place?'

Doctor Morelle gave him the address, adding, 'I have a canine to exercise though I hope to return before you make your departure. Meanwhile, the caretaker's wife will no doubt receive you with her customary hostility, and prove to be stimulatingly obstructive. Goodbye!' He replaced the receiver with a mirthless chuckle.

Detective-Inspector Hood leaned back in his chair and gazed forlornly up at the ceiling through a fog of smoke puffed from his inevitable briar. He tried to analyse what lay behind the Doctor's unusual attitude. Not that he wanted Doctor Morelle to hand him murderers on a metaphorical plate. But it did seem a bit odd that he should have allowed the murderer to get away just so that the busy brains of Scotland Yard could be put to the test. Hood's worried frown became uncreased, and he laughed heartily as he remembered that he'd never slipped up on a single case that had involved Doctor Morelle. The great Doctor must have a card up his sleeve. Perhaps he was deliberately allowing an easy case to complicate itself so that he could display his scientific — what was the word — ratio-something? Anyway it was just a long-winded way of saying 'reasoning'.

The Inspector's conjectures were interrupted by the telephone shrilling again, and he answered it.

'Found in a taxi, eh?' he echoed into the mouthpiece. 'Outside the hospital? What had killed him? Injection. Oh! Where'd the taxi-driver pick 'em up?'

As Hood caught the reply his eyebrows shot upwards and he sat forward with a jerk. 'Taken ill in a hairdresser's in Soho did you say? Well I'll be — Oh, never mind. Keep the body at the hospital and wait for me there.'

Hood rubbed his hands together in satisfaction, as he rose from the desk, and reached for his bowler. 'Well, we've got the body, we know how it was done, and Doctor Morelle can identify the murderer. This *will* be a sitting pigeon!'

A little while later a police car drew up outside the house in which was the empty flat. Detective-Inspector Hood, together with a sergeant and a couple of other officers, had not been in the flat long when Doctor Morelle strolled in, nonchalantly puffing a Le Sphinx. He was followed closely by Miss Frayle, carrying the mongrel terrier in her arms. Hood gave the dog a glance. 'Been taking it for a walk?' he said.

Doctor Morelle motioned Miss Frayle to put the animal down and he stubbed out his cigarette.

'Your deduction is unerringly correct,' he said with mock admiration. 'Or, rather, it might be correct to say the animal took *us* for a perambulation. It appeared distinctly, high-spirited and strangely reluctant to return from the walk — so much so that we had to carry it back. Strange what intelligence mongrels have!'

Hood bit his pipe stem so tightly that he almost snapped it.

'Heavens above!' he exploded. 'A murderer at large — and all you talk about is a dog.'

With a sardonic chuckle the Doctor proceeded to tie up the dog by its lead. It seemed more resigned to being restrained from rushing off, and sat quietly enough watching what was going on about it with one ear cocked, but wearing rather a mournful look.

Doctor Morelle stroked its head mesmerically, and then the Inspector was at his elbow holding out two photographs for him to see.

'Recognise these two?'

The Doctor regarded the photographs shrewdly. Pointing to the left one, he pronounced: 'That was the individual who collapsed suddenly in the tonsorial establishment, and this one — ' indicating the other photograph, 'was the person who posed as a blind man and a doctor in turn.' He regarded Hood through half-closed eyes. 'Both men have police records, I take it?'

The other nodded. 'This one,' and he tapped one of the photos 'is the man you saw apparently taken ill — his name's Zucci — and he is, or rather was, a 'fence'. And this other gentleman, named

Mason, is an expert in the art of cracking safes. Incidentally Zucci's dead — '

'Dead?' echoed Miss Frayle.

'Ah, I feared as much — '

Hood regarded the Doctor through a cloud of smoke from his pipe. 'Mason murdered him. In the taxi you saw them go off in. Unless I'm much mistaken, he'd first of all jabbed a hypodermic into him while they sat next to each other in the barber's shop, and then he got him away to finish him off, afterwards making his getaway.

'The driver — who identified him from his photograph as you have done — says he must have slipped out of the taxi on the way to the hospital. The doctor there said Zucci had received two injections of a powerful drug, the second one proving fatal. As he couldn't have injected himself the second time — he'd still be affected too much by the first shot — I think it's pretty safe to assume it was Mason who pumped him full of poison.'

Doctor Morelle nodded as he ground the stub of his cigarette under his heel and relit another one. 'Your powers of elucidation do you credit,' he murmured.

'Now,' Hood began with a groan, 'you're not going to tell me I'm all wrong?'

'On the contrary,' the Doctor smiled thinly, 'I would hazard that your deduction is singularly accurate. No doubt the murderer, Mason, will confirm your hypothesis.'

'When we catch him!' Hood's pipe bubbled agitatedly. 'He's always been a slippery customer, has Mason. Fellows of his type have dozens of hideouts, and he's a master of disguise. He stretched out his thick, large hands in despair, 'why did you have to let him get away, Doctor?'

Doctor Morelle did not answer. He merely puffed at his cigarette, and a thin smile quirked the corners of his lips.

Miss Frayle pushed in front of him. 'Doctor how can you be so tantalising?' she burst out. 'Why don't you tell the Inspector where he can find Mason and spare his worry?'

'You — you know where Mason is at this moment?' Hood expostulated, his former high spirits returning.

'Indeed yes. Merely five minutes' distance in your automobile,' the Doctor said. 'Argus Court, a small block of flats off Tottenham Court Road. The porter of the building will no doubt inform you as to the number of Mason's flat.'

'He'll know him from the photo we've got.' Hood was already at the door. 'Coming with me, Doctor?'

'I would prefer not to do so. At the moment I have a rather strong desire for intelligent company. I prefer to remain with this canine.'

The Inspector laughed genially, taking the gibe lightly with his usual good nature.

'If our man's there,' he called over his shoulder, 'we shan't be long.'

★   ★   ★

About an hour later, Doctor Morelle, Miss Frayle, and Detective-Inspector Hood, who had returned from Mason's flat, were standing under the glare of the unshaded electric light of the bare, cheerless room. The Doctor was smoking a cigarette, the Inspector sucking at his pipe. He was saying:

'Yes, he was at home all right, though we weren't very welcome callers. However, he was sensible and came quietly enough, and on the way he confessed to the murder.'

'What a dreadful man!' Miss Frayle gasped. 'One doesn't seem to be safe walking about London even in broad daylight. Why, when I was waiting for the Doctor some person came up to me and — '

Doctor Morelle clicked his tongue impatiently, and drowned Miss Frayle's revelations of the London underworld by asking Hood:

'Did he vouchsafe the motive?'

'A sordid sort of story, really. He'd been out of the country for a few months, and while he was away Zucci, whom he'd never actually met, though he'd heard about him, got to know the girl he was in love with and took her away with him.

'He determined to fix him for it — he seems a vindictive sort of fellow — and he hit upon a plan which he thought would enable him to commit the murder without being caught.' He smiled grimly. 'Lots of crooks have had similar ideas.'

He proceeded:

'He discovered that Zucci went to the same hairdresser about once a week. So, hiring this empty flat for a place where he could make a quick change, he disguised himself as a blind beggar and kept a lookout near the hairdressing saloon for his prospective victim.

'When Zucci showed up Mason nipped along here and then went back to put the more unpleasant part of his plan into operation. He might have got away with it, too, might have disappeared without a trace after he'd slipped out of the taxi — only you happened to — well, to decide to have a haircut at about the same time. Incidentally,' he said through a puff of smoke, 'you never told me how you discovered Mason's address, Doctor?'

Doctor Moreile tapped a Le Sphinx on his thin gold case, and regarded the other quizzically.

'Surely I do not need to explain that?'

he retorted in tones of mock surprise. 'It must be obvious, even — '

'Even to a policeman, eh?' Hood finished with a genial laugh. 'Well, it's got me beat. How *did* you do it?'

'Have three guesses, inspector Hood,' Miss Frayle suggested. 'It is really quite simple. I was with the Doctor all the time and — '

'If you really cannot elucidate the problem,' Doctor Morelle interrupted, 'I suppose I shall be compelled to inform you. Quite simply, it was the canine that led me to the murderer's residence. The mongrel pulled at the lead and I merely followed.'

'Well, I'll be blowed! So that's what you meant when you said you preferred intelligent company — the dog's company, eh?' Hood gave a hearty laugh, then he bent his knees and patted the dog's head. 'Poor little blighter,' he muttered. 'Sorry you had to betray your master like you did. But there's some queer people running loose, and sometimes it seems there isn't anything no man nor dog can do about them.'

Doctor Morelle was opening the flat door. His finely chiselled nostrils quivering distastefully.

'I am apt to find your sentimental philosophisings just a little too moving,' he pronounced, 'so with your permission, and if Miss Frayle will kindly stir herself to pedestrian activity, we will take our departure.'

'Right-o, Doctor,' the Inspector called blithely. 'Thanks for all you've done, you've been tremendously helpful — '

But Doctor Morelle was already out of the doorway and on his way up the street, Miss Frayle hurrying after him.

5

THE CASE OF THE
VANISHING FILM STAR

Miss Frayle only occasionally visited a cinema, not that she did not enjoy seeing films, but Doctor Morelle's scathing criticism of them dissuaded her somewhat from going more often.

'Ah, yes, my dear Miss Frayle,' he would murmur sardonically whenever she advised him she planned to spend an hour or two at a cinema, 'indulging in that curious form of escapism so welcomed by the masses.' And he would sigh with over-elaborate concern.

'Aware as I am, of course, of your extraordinarily limited intelligence, nevertheless I cannot refrain from expressing my amazement that even you actually find enjoyment in such a form of so-called relaxation.'

'Oh, but it's quite amusing — ' she

would try to defend herself, but he would cut her protestations short.

'While here in this house,' he would continue, 'you have access to the most engrossing literature written — '. He would cough with an attempt at modesty that caused her to blush with shame on his behalf and proceed. ' — Some of the volumes I have contributed myself would capture your interest far more than any puerile rubbish projected upon a cinema screen. But no, you would prefer to waste your time with hundreds of other cretinous creatures witnessing a shadow-show accompanied by mechanically recorded dialogue and music . . . '

He would cease as if the subject was too pitiably beneath his contempt for him to waste further words. And Miss Frayle always went to see the film she had in mind just the same.

One morning the telephone rang and she felt a thrill of excitement when the voice at the other end asked her if Mr. Sam Keller could speak to the Doctor. Sam Keller, she knew, was the famous film producer, the man who had come all the way from Hollywood to build up the British film producing branch of his American company. He had already constructed enormous studios at Elstree, which swarmed with Hollywood technicians and directors — and some of the most glamorous stars. Sam Keller, the man who could take over an entire floor of the Savoy for himself and his secretaries and retinue, who picked up the telephone and spoke to New York and Hollywood as easily as Miss Frayle might speak to one of the Doctor's patients. Sam Keller, who brought over his own stable of trotting ponies (though he had no time ever in which to watch them trot); Sam Keller, who could pick you out from a crowd and with a wave of his magic wand put your name up in lights all over the world and pay you millions of dollars a year.

Naturally, when she gave the name to Doctor Morelle he disclaimed any knowledge of it. When she gave him some idea of his importance and explained that the great film producer wished to speak to him personally he gave her a contemptuous glance and told her to say he was out.

'His secretary says it's urgent,' she said.

'I am out.'

'But he may be ill. Dying,' she persisted.

He threw her a frosty glance and resumed his work on the contents of his notebook and the other papers before him on his desk. Miss Frayle shrugged in despair and returned to the telephone, She was back in a moment.

'Mr. Keller has spoken to me himself,' she said. 'It is a matter of some importance to him upon which he would be very grateful for your advice . . . ' The Doctor might not have been aware of her presence. She went on: 'Mr. Keller also asked me to tell you he is a personal friend of Mr. Paul Van Piper of New York.'

Doctor Morelle brought up his head quickly.

'Why did you not advise me of that fact at once?' he snapped, and went swiftly to the telephone. Miss Frayle followed him, wishing fervently she could have summoned up sufficient courage to have asked the Doctor how she could possibly have known about Mr. Keller's friendship with Mr. Van Piper until Mr. Keller had told her so himself.

'Doctor Morelle?' a pleasantly soft voice with a Californian accent greeted the Doctor over the telephone.

'Doctor Morelle speaking.'

'I want to ask you about poisoning.'

'What precisely do you wish to know?'

'Well, you see, Doctor, I'm at the moment producing a film called 'The Wonderful Hour'.'

'A highly original title I feel sure!' Doctor Morelle could not refrain from making the sarcastic comment. The other, however, seemed not to detect the sardonic note in the Doctor's tone.

'You like it?' Keller asked. 'Fine! I thought it up myself.' He went on: 'Well now, the point is this — we've just started to film a scene which builds up to a terrific climax in which the girl takes poison. Belladonna.'

'A deliriant often favoured by women of a somewhat hysterical and neurotic nature,' observed Doctor Morelle.

'Er — something like that,' said Keller uncertainly. 'I said to make it Belladonna because I liked the sound of the name.'

'Would you mind informing me exactly in what way all this can possibly concern me?'

'You see, after the woman's taken the poison — the woman in the film, that is — we want to make sure she reacts in the right way.'

Doctor Morelle permitted himself a mirthless chuckle.

'My dear Mr. Keller, any handbook on elementary first-aid will give you all the facts you require concerning the symptoms — widely dilated pupils, delirium . . .' He broke off with some irritation. 'Really, you're wasting my time. Go out and purchase the first book you can find on the subject. You will discover the reactions to an overdose of Atropa Belladonna set forth in detail. A child could understand it.'

'Maybe,' said the other grimly, 'but Lilli Lagrande is no child!'

'Lilli who?'

'Lilli Lagrande, star of the picture — she plays the part of the woman who's got to take the poison.'

'If, as I gather from your tone, this person is unable to conform to the instructions given her regarding the performance of a simple action, then surely the obvious procedure is to secure someone else with a trifle more intelligence,' advised Doctor Morelle with some impatience.

Keller chuckled.

'You don't quite understand. Lilli is one of my big stars. Her pictures clean up. But she has to have every line, every movement, every turn of the head hammered into her. Now d'you see what I'm driving at?'

'I must confess I am not very well acquainted with your business methods, Mr. Keller.'

'Look, she won't take any advice on all this poison stuff from the director of the film. Says he knows nothing about it. She won't even let me try and show her. But if I take a big doctor down to the studios — somebody like — well, like the great Doctor Morelle, for instance — she'll just eat out of your hand.'

'That eccentric experience I have no wish to enjoy,' replied the Doctor, not displeased, nevertheless, by the other's flattery.

'Now, Doctor,' pleaded Keller. 'You can name your own fee — all expenses paid — and whatever figure you say I'll double it. It'll only take you a couple of hours in the morning. It may sound a crazy notion to you, but it's important as hell to me.'

Doctor Morelle hesitated before deciding to give a negative reply.

'You're the only man in the wide world can help me,' urged Keller, 'just as you were the only man who was able to help our mutual friend Paul Van Piper. You saved his wife's life . . . '

The Doctor could not repress a thin smile at the other's anxiety, and the reminder of one of his greatest triumphs caused him to pause a moment longer in reflection.

'Very well,' he said in a tone of great reluctance amounting to condescension.

'That's great! I'll send a car to pick you up at ten in the morning.'

Miss Frayle, who had contrived to follow the gist of the conversation with suppressed excitement, could hardly refrain from applauding the Doctor's decision.

The following morning as they drove in the luxurious limousine past the imposing entrance to the Excelsior Studios at Elstree, Doctor Morelle observed rather acidly to Miss Frayle: 'I trust this visit will afford you an opportunity to become disillusioned concerning these motion pictures which you are continually eulogising, instead of expending a little concentration upon more edifying matters.'

'Oh, yes, Doctor Morelle,' she replied, having heard not one word he had spoken. She was far too absorbed in her surroundings, and thrilled with the exciting possibility that perhaps one of Hollywood's glamorous images viewed hitherto from the darkness of a cinema might appear startlingly in the flesh before her gaze. She fiddled with her spectacles, polishing them in eager anticipation.

They entered a large, modern white

building, and were conducted at once to Mr. Keller's office. Surrounded by chromium-plated furniture and rugs and curtains, which must have cost a small fortune, Doctor Morelle concluded the film producer was a man not without certain good taste. He had the rather disconcerting habit, however, of keeping a light-coloured Fedora hat perched on the back of his head. He was relieved to see that he did not have a cigar stuck in his mouth.

Keller seemed very glad to see them, and proposed to conduct them to the 'set' right away. Before they left the office, he depressed a switch and spoke into the instrument on his desk:

'I shall be on Stage Number Four — and don't interrupt me!'

'Yes, Mr. Keller,' came the tinny reply. As they came out in the corridor, they heard several loud speakers announce:

'Mr. Keller's on Number Four . . . Mr. Keller's on Number Four . . . '

'A little premature, surely,' suggested Doctor Morelle.

'Take no notice of that — it's

customary in the motion picture business to keep your name in front of folks, or they're liable to forget you're about!' he explained mildly with an almost apologetic smile.

They came into the open air, crossed a square and entered a huge structure covered with long sloping roofs. A red electric bulb glowed outside the door, and several notices adjured their silence. These instructions Mr. Keller ignored, talking the whole time in his smooth, soft accent, as they picked their way through a wilderness of electric cables and odd 'props' towards the group of actors on the brilliantly illuminated set. The building reverberated with the banging of workmen's hammers, until a voice called:

'Quiet!'

Whereupon a little man in a loud tie and a louder pullover leapt to his feet and shouted energetically:

'Quiet on the set!'

The hammering ceased, and immediately silence fell upon the crowd of technicians, actors and others grouped around the garishly illuminated scene.

'Lights!'

The brilliant lighting was approximately trebled.

'Roll 'em . . . Camera!'

Miss Frayle watched with bated breath while the two sun-tan complexioned actors sprang into life, followed by the long arm of the ubiquitous microphone and an ever-following camera while they moved round the set.

Just as she was becoming interested in the scene, a voice called: 'Cut!'

The little man in the bright pullover leapt up again and yelled:

'Save 'em!'

Five arc lamps snapped into darkness, and again the pandemonium of hammering broke out. Miss Frayle goggling, found it hard to believe that out of the apparent muddle and chaos before her and which seemed to prevail on every side, could anything evolve which she, in company with cinema patrons the world over would pay to see.

She glanced at the Doctor. His saturnine features wore their most supercilious expression as he gazed with studied disinterest at nothing in particular.

'That's Lilli Lagrande,' whispered Miss Frayle to him when Keller had left them for a moment to speak to the director of the film. 'She's French . . . and that's Anthony Bell with her . . . the papers call him the new British star.' She had seen them both in several films and felt a thrill as she recognised them. The Doctor hardly deigned to glance in their direction.

'By a cursory glance at their respective crania, I should say they were both of a singularly low order of intelligence,' he murmured unkindly, and deliberately employing, as he well knew, only a small degree of accuracy.

After a moment there were more shouts for silence, the lights came on again in all their brilliance, the man in the multi-coloured shirt shouted. Miss Frayle watched the petite blonde and glamorous French star, brought to England after a dazzlingly successful stay in Hollywood, whence she had gone after her triumphs in French films. At the moment she was going through the antics and emotions befitting a society butterfly who has fallen in love with a poor but handsome young sculptor. Anthony Bell, with appropriately streamlined profile and dark crinkly hair, portrayed the sculptor. As Lilli Lagrande passionately declared she had at last found true love in his arms, Miss Frayle heard a cockney voice, a man's, mutter behind her:

'Conceited little pup, he is,' said the voice.

Another man voiced a cockney agreement. 'S'right,' said the second voice. 'All 'e thinks of all the time is gettin' 'is pretty-pretty dial in the papers!'

'Ar,' said the voice number one. 'Fair makes yer sick it does!'

Miss Frayle glanced round, but the two men, they appeared to be studio workmen, had moved off. She glanced at Doctor Morelle to see if he might also have heard perhaps and been amused by the scrap of conversation. But his face was as disinterested as ever. She turned to the scene before her again. It seemed to be about to end.

Presently Keller returned, bringing with him the director of the film, another American named Al Palmer.

'Now I'll leave you two together to figure out this poison business,' smiled Keller benevolently, after he had introduced them. 'I got a conference to attend at twelve.' He glanced at his wristwatch. 'See you later, Doctor.'

In spite of the director's loud attire, Doctor Morelle found Palmer quite a reasonable individual, who fired a series of questions at him while a stenographer took down the Doctor's replies

'All right,' said Palmer presently, 'we'll shoot the poison scene.'

'The poison scene!' yelled somebody, and the cry was taken up by a number of other voices.

'First, before we start, Doctor Morelle,' said Palmer, 'I want you to meet Miss Lagrande.' He turned and called quietly: 'Lilli . . . Lilli . . . come on over and meet Doctor Morelle.'

While Miss Frayle watched goggle-eyed, Lilli Lagrande came over and extended a slim beautiful hand to the

Doctor. Introducing them, Palmer went on: 'He's an expert in this Belladonna business, Lilli . . . '

'Ah, Doctor Morelle, I am so glad to see you. Now at last we will get this scene right. Already we have taken it five — six times, but each time something tells me it is wrong. Now, once and for all, we get it right, eh?' Her accent was most attractive, her voice throatily alluring, her smile brilliant, as she looked up at Doctor Morelle.

'I hope so, indeed,' he replied. 'My time is extremely valuable, and I have a consultation immediately after lunch.'

She gave him a wide-eyed look and pouted. Then Palmer was edging her back to the set with final instructions before they began work on the important scene. After delays for various reasons the poison scene began.

But it seemed that the French star had been more than a little optimistic. She was herself mainly to blame. She had an irritating habit of forgetting all the actions and reactions drilled into her by Palmer, and devising touches of her own that were quite inaccurate when the scene was actually shot. As time wore on, tempers became more frayed, and even Miss Frayle decided Lilli Lagrande really was not over-gifted with intelligence. The Doctor was frankly bored, and took little pains to conceal it.

When a bell outside the building rang shrilly to announce to everyone's relief it was lunchtime, the poison sequence still had a long way to go.

'What can you do with a woman like that?' Palmer said in disgust to the Doctor, as the workmen tramped noisily out of the building. 'No wonder she drove Hollywood crackers! That fellow Bell may get under your skin with his conceit, but he does remember what you tell him. You'll have lunch with me Doctor?'

Doctor Morelle shook his head. 'I must return to town at once. I have an important appointment. If you will kindly direct me to Mr. Keller's office, I will explain to him.'

'Too bad you have to go,' said Palmer, and he gave Miss Frayle a friendly grin. 'Hope we'll be seeing you again.'

'I think that is hardly likely,' said the Doctor firmly.

'Well, anyway, we've got all the technical details fixed now,' said Palmer. 'Thanks to you. And Lilli won't be able to say it isn't the real thing, knowing as she does you were here on the spot to give us the correct reaction stuff and all that. Thanks a lot. You can't imagine what a headache it's been.'

'I rather imagine I can!' murmured the Doctor with a thin smile. The other gave him a quick look and then laughed outright. 'I guess you can, too!' He shook hands genially with them both and then directed the Doctor and Miss Frayle to Keller's office. They made their way through the same heavy, soundproof door by which they had entered the stage, and found themselves in the main corridor. Doctor Morelle and Miss Frayle set off in the direction Al Palmer had given them. It was Miss Frayle who saw the scrap of white against the wall where it had been kicked aside. She picked it up. It was a tiny handkerchief, perfumed and initialled in one corner: 'L.L.'

'Must be Miss Lagrande's,' she said to Doctor Morelle.

'Quite the little Sherlock Holmes!' was his only comment.

She looked round for someone to whom she might hand it over, but there was nobody near. Clutching the handkerchief in her hand, she followed Doctor Morelle hesitantly. They came to a point where another corridor cut across the one along which they were proceeding. They turned left as instructed by Palmer. Some few yards along Miss Frayle's eye caught sight of a door with a silver star painted on it. Beneath the star was the name: LILLI LAGRANDE. She halted, looking at the handkerchief.

'Do you think I might take it in to her?' she asked Doctor Morelle.

'I have no doubt she will be delighted to receive it from you,' he said sarcastically. 'Though whether such a moronic creature will recognise the initials as her own is a debatable point.'

She stood indecisively outside the star-marked door. 'Do not stand there like someone in a trance, perform your errand as quickly as possible and rejoin me in Keller's office,' the Doctor snapped irritably and strode off. So rapidly did he proceed that he bumped into a large, moon-faced young woman who was hurrying down the corridor. Complaining bitterly about the inability of people to watch where they were proceeding, he went off with long raking strides. The young woman stared after him, her mouth open with fright.

This incident inspired Miss Frayle into action, and with a sympathetic smile towards the large young woman, she knocked at the door. As she stood waiting, glancing at the crushed morsel of linen and lace she held, a voice that sounded as if it might be the film star's told her to come in. Lilli Lagrande lay upon a large pink sofa, and was wrapped so far as Miss Frayle could judge in a great cloud of pink feathers. She was alone in the dressing room and surveyed her with great round and very blue eyes over a small parcel, which she was in the act of undoing.

'Oo are you? What do you want?'

Miss Frayle stammered and held out the handkerchief. 'Er — excuse me, Miss Lagrande — ' She wondered desperately if she should not have addressed her as 'Mademoiselle,' after all she was French ' — er — but I found this out there — '.

'You find what out where?'

'Your handkerchief, I think.'

She extended her small soft white hand and took it from her. 'It is mine, yes,' she nodded. 'Thank you very much for bringing it to me.'

Miss Frayle wriggled with nervous excitement. And then she wondered how she could take her leave.

Lilli Lagrande gave her a bewitching smile. 'Perhaps you could untie this parcel for me, pliz? My maid she has gone to lunch . . . It is such a nuisance . . . '

'Why, of course,' and Miss Frayle took the parcel and proceeded quickly and deftly to untie the string.

'That is so kind of you.' And the smile became more brilliant as the wrapping was removed to reveal a cardboard box of attractive design. She took it from Miss Frayle with a gurgle of delight, negligently throwing the visiting card which accompanied it on the floor, after a perfunctory glance at it.

'It is lovely perfume he give me,' she exclaimed, opening the box and taking out a luxurious-looking, beautifully cut bottle and glancing at the gilt label. ''Serenade in the Night' it is call — I have never tried any of this sort before.' She took out the stopper. 'Ahh — !' she breathed ecstatically.

Miss Frayle's nostrils quivered as the clingingly heavy exotic scent was wafted in her direction. She thought it was a decidedly sickly odour. But she said: 'Very nice,' politely. She wondered what Doctor Morelle's reactions would be if he caught her using such an exotic perfume.

'You must have some,' said Lilli Lagrande generously, at that very moment. To her dismay, Miss Frayle realised she could not possibly refuse without offending her. 'Oh, it is *merveilleuse!*' cried the other, liberally dabbing her neck and behind her ears with the contents of the bottle, and shaking some drops on to a handkerchief. 'Give me your handkerchief,' she said.

Apprehensively she did so, and Lilli Lagrande sprinkled it generously with the scent. The air in the dressing room was now heavy with the powerful aroma, and Miss Frayle was thankful when the film star relaxed languidly on her cloud of feathers and waved a hand in dismissal.

'You have to go?' she pouted. 'Such a peety. Goodbye. Shut the door gently please, I have a headache.'

Miss Frayle went out quietly, and took a deep breath of comparatively fresh air. She made her way somewhat unsteadily along the corridor in the direction of Mr. Keller's office. There, she found the Doctor fuming, as he paced up and down. It seemed that the great producer had not returned from his conference, though secretaries continually looked in to inform Doctor Morelle: 'Mr. Keller is expected any minute.'

'Where have you been all this time, Miss Frayle?' he demanded. 'You have had ample opportunity to return lost handkerchiefs of the entire personnel of the studios!'

'I'm sorry, Doctor — Miss Lagrande

— er — detained me — '

He raised his thin aquiline nose and sniffed.

'What a disgustingly heavy perfume there is in here!' He suddenly turned a piercing gaze on her. 'I hope,' he said with a sardonic expression indicating he was already aware she was responsible, 'you can in no way be connected with this peculiarly oriental aroma?'

'It was a present to Miss Lagrande from one of her admirers,' explained Miss Frayle desperately. 'She made me take some.'

'And of course you lacked the moral courage to refuse? You will kindly remain at a reasonable distance so long as that clinging and revoltingly penetrative odour persists.'

'Yes, Doctor Morelle,' said Miss Frayle miserably, and humbly removing herself to a distant corner of the room. At that moment Sam Keller hurried in. He waved aside the Doctor's protests with an apologetic smile.

'Now, now Doctor, I haven't forgotten you have a consultation this afternoon.

You'll be in plenty of time — I've arranged for the studio car to take you wherever you want to go — and we've a chance to eat in here before you start. I've ordered it to be sent in right away.'

Almost as soon as he had spoken, the door opened to admit a waitress carrying a large tray.

Keller beckoned to Miss Frayle.

'Come on over here, Miss Frayle, don't sulk in the corner!' he grinned. 'Help set the table.'

He sniffed appreciatively. 'That's nice perfume you're using,' he declared. 'You must tell me the name, I'll buy my wife some.'

Miss Frayle gave him a shy little smile of gratitude.

When they were sitting around a most appetising lunch, Keller turned to Doctor Morelle and asked:

'Well, how did you get on with Lilli?'

'I regret to say I consider her to be a somewhat cretinous creature,' declared Doctor Morelle acidly.

Keller laughed. 'I've been having a word with Palmer — he says you've got the whole business straightened now anyway. He can go right ahead now he knows the layout. He'll worry Lilli till she delivers the goods.'

'That I feel sure should prove very gratifying!'

Keller pushed his hat back on his head, and sighed.

'If you knew the worry I have over that woman. We've been getting threatening letters for weeks. One came just now demanding five thousand pounds by this morning or she would disappear!'

'You — you mean a threat to kidnap her?' gulped Miss Frayle.

'That's the idea, and then where would my picture be?'

'I should think it might show a considerable improvement!' commented Doctor Morelle.

Keller shook his head. 'You don't know this business, Doctor. Lilli Lagrande's got the goods. We know it. She knows it.'

'Is the — er — lady concerned aware of these letters being sent?' asked the Doctor disinterestedly.

'No. I decided it wouldn't help at all.

She'd get in a state of jitters.'

'I could prescribe a course of extreme physical exertion,' mused Doctor Morelle, 'that would doubtless rid her of some of her temperamental excesses . . . '

The film producer shook his head. 'It's her temperament we want. It's what the public wants, too. So long as we can keep it within limits. I've been handling stars like her for years — it's not too tough when you know how. Keep a tight rein, but not too tight. Know when to tick 'em off, when to encourage 'em, when to — '

The loudspeaker telephone on his desk clicked.

He pressed down a switch.

'What is it?'

'Mr. Keller — Miss Lagrande . . . ' The voice was urgent, almost incoherent. 'Well?'

'She's disappeared,' came the voice from the instrument. 'Her maid went to get her some lunch. When she came back Miss Lagrande had vanished.'

Miss Frayle choked.

'My God!' exclaimed Keller. He stood up for a moment nonplussed, then pressed the switch again.

'Tell Collins to come here right away — and Palmer. And keep your mouth shut,' he snapped.

'Yes, Mr. Keller.'

Collins, who was Keller's right-hand man, proved to be a tall, alert individual in the early thirties. He arrived with Palmer in less than five minutes. As they came in, Doctor Morelle was just intimating that he was about to take his leave. The harassed producer waved him back.

'No, no, Doctor, can't you wait a moment? Maybe you could help us on this? I've heard how you solved some cases, long after the police had given up. I'm against yelling for the police unless it's absolutely necessary — maybe you could solve this case before we call 'em in!'

Collins and Palmer looked at Doctor Morelle anxiously. Palmer said, not very hopefully: 'Maybe it's a false alarm — maybe she's only taking a walk in the park.'

'She hardly looks the type of person

who would go for a country walk,' said the Doctor. 'However, perhaps you would be good enough to inform me who knew about these threatening letters.'

'Just the three of us,' replied Keller decisively. The other two men nodded.

'Who first made the discovery Miss Lagrande was missing?'

'I did,' replied Collins. 'I went along to her dressing room to see her about one or two matters, and found only her maid there. She said she'd brought Miss Lagrande's lunch, and it was getting cold She'd no idea where Lilli was. I got into touch with one or two likely people, but they hadn't seen her. Then I remembered about those letters, so I thought I'd better tell Mr. Keller's secretary to get through here.'

The producer nodded approvingly. He turned to Doctor Morelle. 'Any other questions you want to ask, Doctor?'

The Doctor shook his head negatively, and, warned to say nothing about what had occurred, Collins returned to his own department

Keller said to Palmer:

'Now, Al, tell us what you know about this — '

He was interrupted by the door opening suddenly to admit Anthony Bell, his wavy hair somewhat awry, and a peculiar expression on his made-up features.

'I've been threatened!' he announced in a voice a shade too high-pitched. He waved a letter.

'What — you as well?' Keller snapped at him.

The young actor's handsome face took on a puzzled look.

'Why?' he began, 'has somebody else — ?'

'Lagrande's disappeared,' said Keller. 'Kidnapped, we think. But for God's sake, keep it to yourself. What's this letter of yours?'

He took the letter from Bell, then unlocked and opened a drawer in his desk and offered several others for Doctor Morelle's inspection.

'Where did you find your communication?' the Doctor asked the young actor.

'On my dressing room table. It was

there when I came off the set. I expect it's a joke of some sort really . . . ' He smiled as if to dismiss it after all as a matter of little importance.

Doctor Morelle lighted a Le Sphinx. He said through a cloud of cigarette smoke: 'Are you suggesting now that this is perhaps not so important after all?'

Anthony Bell seemed to grow even more uncomfortable. He looked at the door as if undecided whether to stay or go. Miss Frayle, who had remained in the background during the discussion between the Doctor, the producer and the others, decided the young man's face was really somewhat displeasing when viewed at close quarters. She recalled the conversation she had overheard between the two cockney workmen, and agreed to herself they had been right about the actor. His face was full of conceit, and there seemed to be something more evident in his expression now, she decided. There seemed to be a shadow of fear across it. He was answering Doctor Morelle with ill-assumed composure.

'Well . . . no, I shouldn't think so. After

all, I get dozens of odd sorts of letters — '

He spread his hands expansively as if to indicate the volume of his fan mail. Doctor Morelle mentally reached the conclusion the young man was, at any rate, a singularly indifferent actor out of his professional environment however adequate a performer he might be in it.

'Such a letter might result in some quite advantageous publicity,' he murmured in a quiet, insinuating tone. There was a silence for a few moments. Then Bell coughed and grinned sheepishly.

'Well, I expect you'll be busy with this other job,' he murmured.

'Did you see anything of Miss Lagrande when you came off the set?' asked Keller.

'Good heavens, no! My dressing room's in the opposite block. Besides, off the set we're not speaking.'

Keller could not refrain from exchanging a grin with Palmer, as Anthony Bell made a comparatively unobtrusive exit.

'Well, what d'you make of that?' asked Keller.

'It rather looks as if Mr. Bell, unaware of an apparently real danger threatening

Miss Lagrande, was seeking rather more than his fair share of publicity,' said Doctor Morelle.

'Just the kinda trick he'd go for,' declared Palmer contemptuously. 'The swollen-headed dummy!'

'He's got a nerve!' chuckled Keller, glancing again at the note Bell had left behind. 'Fancy putting his price at ten thousand. Does he really imagine we'd pay that to save having him kidnapped?'

'Your guess is as good as mine, Mr. Keller,' grinned Palmer.

'Maybe I should have a serious talk to that guy,' murmured Keller. 'Now, Al, what d'you know about this Lagrande business?'

Palmer shook his head.

'Not a thing — but I hope she turns up pretty soon. We're two days behind schedule. And I'm due back on that set right now.' Keller looked across at Doctor Morelle who nodded.

'All right, Al,' the producer said. 'We know where to find you. Better shoot one or two of those scenes which don't include Lilli.' He spent a few moments indicating the nature of the work Palmer could proceed with during the film actress's absence.

When he had gone, Keller lowered himself into his revolving chair with a sigh.

'As if I haven't had enough worries with this so-and-so picture! Trouble with the story, trouble with the title, the cast, the sets, and now Lilli has to go and get herself kidnapped!' He gave his hat a vicious tug that pulled it over one eye.

Miss Frayle smiled at him sympathetically.

'Try not to worry, Mr. Keller,' she said. 'I'm sure we'll get her back for you safely — that is, if Miss Lagrande really has got lost.'

'Thanks, Miss Frayle,' smiled the American somewhat wanly.

'Might we not take a look at Miss Lagrande's dressing room?' suggested Doctor Morelle. 'It would be as well if you remained here, Mr. Keller, in the event of any fresh news materialising.'

Keller nodded, his face brightening a little.

'I'll get my secretary to take you along.'

He pressed a button, and a stalwart, moon-faced young woman entered. Miss Frayle and Doctor Morelle recalled simultaneously that she was the young woman he had bumped into in the corridor a little earlier.

'Take Doctor Morelle and Miss Frayle to Miss Lagrande's room,' Keller instructed her.

'Yes. Mr. Keller,' she answered in a colourless voice.

As they were going, Keller recalled her and handed over a sheaf of papers. 'On your way back, call in and give these production schedules to Mr. Collins, and ask him to check with all departments.'

'Yes. Mr. Keller.'

She led Doctor Morelle and Miss Frayle out into the corridor, and eventually they came once more to the dressing room of the missing film star.

'There are only four other rooms in this corridor,' noted Doctor Morelle, eyeing the secretary. 'Could you inform me who occupies these rooms?'

'Well . . . ' the girl thought for a

moment, 'next to Miss Lagrande is — '
She mentioned the name of a well-known
character actress, and rattled off the
names of two other actresses who used
the dressing rooms. One of them was not
at the studio that day, she added.

'And the fourth room?'

'Empty just now.' The secretary opened
the door of Miss Lagrande's room. They
were greeted by an overwhelming waft of
the inevitable perfume. Morelle turned to
the young woman. 'There is no need for
you to wait,' he said.

The secretary muttered something and
hurried back along the corridor towards
Keller's offices.

When the door closed, Doctor Morelle
began a careful examination of the room.
There were some signs of a struggle. Two
pots of vanishing cream had been
overturned. Cosmetic bottles had been
swept to the floor; so had the ornate
bottle containing the perfume, 'Serenade
in the Night'.

The Doctor picked up this bottle and
sniffed at it thoughtfully and with
considerable repugnance.

'Miss Frayle, you were probably the last person to see Miss Lagrande before she was abducted. I feel certain you have a number of helpful theories to put forward regarding the matter?'

Miss Frayle ignored the sardonic tone of his voice and looked completely bewildered.

'I — I can't understand it,' she stammered. 'I — I — don't know what to think. It — It's all so strange.'

He smiled frostily. 'You surprise and disappoint me,' he murmured. 'I had hoped for sensational revelations,' and he sighed elaborately. Then he said: 'The person who perpetrated this abduction is still at large and on the premises. That much I have ascertained.'

Miss Frayle's eyes widened in alarm behind her spectacles.

The Doctor chuckled at her expression of apprehension.

'Do not distress yourself, Miss Frayle. Let us proceed to investigate the adjoining dressing rooms.'

She followed him out and along to the next dressing room. He tried the door and looked inside. It was a room similar to Lilli Lagrande's, though very much less ornately and expensively furnished, and not so large. The same applied to the other dressing rooms. Then they came to the end room, which the secretary had described as unused. The door was locked. Doctor Morelle paused and eyed the door reflectively.

'Shall I get the key, Doctor?'

'No, Miss Frayle. You remain here. I will obtain it myself. No doubt the secretary who conducted us here will have some idea as to its whereabouts.'

He made his way back along the corridor.

The moon-faced young woman's office proved to be a small room, crowded with files. The girl was typing rapidly, amidst stacks of papers and documents of every description on her desk. The walls were smothered with photographs of film actresses.

'I wish to have the key of the end dressing room, which you described to me as empty,' he said to her. She looked surprised for a moment, then recovered.

'Oh yes, I forgot to mention it's usually kept locked. There should be a key somewhere, in the commissionaire's office I expect.'

'You have no duplicates?'

She appeared to ponder his question for a moment, then opened a drawer and produced a small bunch of keys. Each was labelled, and she finally selected one.

'I think you will find that's it.'

He thanked her and returned to Miss Frayle.

The empty dressing room was dusty, and contained little of interest. It was very much like the other rooms except that it had an emergency exit which led out to the back of that part of the studio. Doctor Morelle looked round and then suddenly stepped forward and picked up a large piece of curtain, old and faded, which had been carelessly thrown on top of a large locker. He pulled it off and threw it on to the floor. Miss Frayle saw his eyes narrow as he bent and sniffed. She noticed four large holes in the lid of the locker, which was fastened with a small padlock. Doctor Morelle looked round quickly and indicated a large chisel lying on a table by the door. It had obviously been left behind by a forgetful workman. Miss Frayle handed it to him. Inserting it under the lid, the Doctor managed to burst it open without much difficulty.

Within lay Lilli Lagrande, gagged, bound and unconscious.

'Miss Lagrande!' gasped Miss Frayle, goggling.

'Brandy quickly!' snapped Doctor Morelle, quickly unfastening the cords that bound the film star. Miss Frayle rushed out of the room and almost collided with Keller's secretary.

'Brandy — for Miss Lagrande,' gasped Miss Frayle.

The young woman stared at her in amazement. Then she pulled herself together.

'I'll get it — come with me — ' she said.

By the time Miss Frayle had returned, Lilli Lagrande was moaning and seemed to be recovering consciousness.

'Did you happen to see Mr. Keller's secretary?' was Doctor Morelle's first question as he took the brandy and held it to the actress's lips.

'Mr. Keller's secretary? I — I don't know — I think she went back to her office. It was she who got the brandy for me,' explained Miss Frayle.

'Then go and find Mr. Keller immediately and advise him to detain the young woman!' Doctor Morelle snapped.

Miss Frayle stared at him in blank amazement.

'Det — detain her?' she gulped. 'But what for? Why — ?'

'If you would restrain yourself from asking futile questions and carry out my instructions at once I should be better pleased.'

'Yes, Doctor Morelle, of course.' And, completely in a daze Miss Frayle hurried off in search of the film producer.

A little while later, Doctor Morelle was saying to Keller:

'Your secretary's idea was to keep Miss Lagrande in that locker until tonight. Then, under cover of darkness, bundle her into her little two-seater car, via the emergency exit which leads from that dressing room, and take her to her bungalow where she lives alone.'

Keller pushed his hat on to the back of his head with a groan. 'But what beats me,' he said, 'is why she should do all this. Threatening letters . . . Kidnapping . . . It's fantastic!'

Doctor Morelle smiled sardonically.

'It may not occur to you, but the world in which she works is somewhat fantastic! Undoubtedly it finally affected her mind. The young woman is obviously unbalanced. Witnessing these — er — strange creatures around her incessantly gave her a craving for fame, or notoriety. Being a secretary offered her practically no opportunity to fulfil this ambition, therefore she was forced to evolve some plan by which she could achieve the desired-for publicity.'

Keller nodded thoughtfully.

'So that's how it was? Well, we were damned lucky she didn't suffocate Lilli in that locker.'

'Yes, that would have been even more unpleasant for both the young woman and Miss Lagrande,' said Doctor Morelle.

'Not only that — my film would have been ruined!' declared Keller emphatically.

★　★　★

On the way back to London in the luxurious car, Miss Frayle remained deep in thought until they reached the outer suburbs.

'I still can't see how you came to suspect that girl, Doctor Morelle,' she said at last.

Doctor Morelle lit a Le Sphinx.

'What was the name given to that perfume used by that moronic creature, the aroma of which still pervades the atmosphere about you?'

'You mean 'Serenade in the Night'?'

He received the information in silence. Then he mused: 'Yes . . . Quite the most pungent aroma I have encountered for a considerable time. However — ' he smiled thinly as he went on, ' — it's an ill wind that blows nobody any good! But for that scent I might have taken longer to suspect the secretary of being concerned in the abduction.'

Miss Frayle stared at him, not grasping the significance of what he was saying. He went on smoothly:

'When first she came into Mr. Keller's office, I imagined I received a fresh waft of the perfume, but could not be positive you were not still responsible for it. When, however, I visited her later in her own office, the matter was placed beyond any doubt. I argued, therefore, the young woman must have followed you into Miss Lagrande's dressing room, for I had already collided with her in the corridor just after you left me to visit Miss Lagrande. At that time she was certainly free of the perfume, or I should have noticed it. It was during her struggle with Miss Lagrande that the bottle was overturned and some of the scent precipitated on to her attire.'

'So that was it,' murmured Miss Frayle, reconstructing the events in her mind.

'As you so succinctly phrase it, my dear Miss Frayle, 'that was it'. A perfectly simple matter of ratiocination that you, no doubt, confidently feel anyone could elucidate! After all, it needs only shrewd perception, a gift — one might almost say, genius — for collating the facts as they present themselves to the observer . . . '

Miss Frayle sighed as Doctor Morelle launched into one of his moods of self-commiseration. She closed her eyes. The speeding car hummed onwards and the sardonic voice in her ear became a blurred sound that gradually drifted further and further away.

When Doctor Morelle paused in his tirade to demand of her why she made no answer, he observed that she was asleep, her spectacles half-way down her nose, a little smile touching her lips.

'What a careless young woman!' he murmured in a tone of exasperation. 'If they were to break she would be unable to perform her work — doubtless she has omitted to provide herself with a spare pair.' Leaning forward, he gently replaced her spectacles to their proper position on Miss Frayle's nose.

6

THE CASE OF THE FINAL CURTAIN

Slowly the man backed across the room, horror and entreaty in his face, his eyes wide and staring. Still the woman advanced, the sinister black revolver pointed at him, her attitude grim and purposeful.

'No, no you wouldn't!' the man sobbed. 'You can't shoot!'

'D'you think I haven't the courage to kill you?'

'No! No! Put away that gun! I beg you — let — let's talk this over calmly — '

'The time for talking is finished!'

'Listen to me . . . ' But she cut him short. Brutally and deliberately she said:

'You're going to die.'

'Listen! Please listen — !'

He was on his knees now, grovelling at her feet. She shot him as he held out his hands towards her in a last appeal. He stared at her, his jaw sagging as if in surprise, and then he fell forward on his face. There followed a moment's breathless silence.

And then — as the curtain slowly fell — a thunderous wave of applause surged on to the stage from the packed theatre.

Miss Frayle sniffed her smelling salts clasped tightly in her hand for the nth time. Doctor Morelle shifted impatiently in his seat, and his supercilious glance swept the applauding audience around him. He turned to observe Miss Frayle as she fumbled with the stopper of her smelling salts, sniffing convulsively as she did so.

'My dear Miss Frayle,' he murmured viciously in her ear, 'if you must use stimulants so often, could you not contrive to do so with a little less sound accompaniment?'

'I — I can't help it,' she gulped. 'You — you shouldn't have made me c-come to this aw-awful play!' And she gave a long and shuddering sniff.

He bestowed a look of disgust and

displeasure on her.

'Hysterical nonsense!' he snapped.

Doctor Morelle had but little taste for theatre entertainment, but the play he had decided to witness this particular evening was one that had appealed to him purely from a scientific aspect. It was, in fact, a play of a somewhat macabre nature. It had captured the interest and purse of the public, and was one of the most phenomenal successes the London Theatre had known for a long time.

It had occurred to the Doctor that the effects of vicarious horrifics viewed at close quarters upon the human mind might be worthy of some study. Accordingly, he had cast about for a subject whom he might put to the test. He had failed to hit upon the person whom he felt would most suitably react to the experiment — until he realised with some sudden sardonic satisfaction that none other than Miss Frayle would be ideal for the purpose.

He had, of course, discreetly omitted to acquaint her of the fact he had chosen her because of his considered opinion that she might be of some value to him in the role of a human 'guinea-pig', and had prevailed upon her to accompany him to a performance. As the close of Act II approached he was seriously beginning to regret his choice, for Miss Frayle seemed to have had recourse to her smelling-salts more frequently than he could have imagined possible. Her continued sniffing allied to the, to him, appalling credulity of the audience who were lapping up as puerile a farrago of futile nonsense as he had ever encountered, grated upon him with increasing irritation. His lip curling with open distaste, he once more surveyed the people about him who were still applauding with almost hysterical vigour the end of the second act. He was about to raise a hand to stifle a deliberately ostentatious yawn, when suddenly the applause faltered and subsided.

Miss Frayle was tugging at his elbow.

'Doctor Morelle!' she whispered. 'Who — who's the man who's just come in front of the curtain?'

He glanced up as a man with greying

hair and in evening dress stood before the purple stage curtain and held up a hand for silence. His face was troubled and grave.

'Ladies and gentlemen,' he said. The auditorium was now deathly silent. 'Ladies and gentlemen . . . Your attention, please. If there is a doctor present would he please come round immediately? I — I regret to state there has been an accident . . .'

'Doctor Morelle!' gasped Miss Frayle.

He drew his lips together in a thin line of displeasure.

'There is almost sure to be another member of the medical profession present,' he murmured, glancing round. But if there was another doctor in the theatre he apparently preferred to remain anonymous. After a short pause, Doctor Morelle rose irritably to his feet and moved towards the end of the row of stalls where he and Miss Frayle had their seats. Hundreds of faces watched them as Miss Frayle followed him.

The Doctor appeared oblivious of the intense interest in him as, without condescending to apologise, he made his way quickly through the audience. Miss Frayle blundered short-sightedly in his wake, tripping over feet and ankles and apologising profusely as she tried to keep up with him. They were directed through a small door at the side, up a short flight of steps and through another door on to the side of the stage. The man who had appeared before the curtain greeted Doctor Morelle with undisguised agitation.

'It's Gerald Winters!' he said.

'That's the actor who was shot in the play?' asked Miss Frayle.

The man, who had introduced himself as the stage-director, was leading them through a door that opened off the stage on to a short passage.

'Yes,' he nodded. Then to the Doctor: 'He's in here.'

He pushed open the dressing room door. Doctor Morelle crossed over to a narrow couch on which the inert figure of the actor lay. His make-up was incongruous and ghastly on a face that was grey beneath. Miss Frayle shuddered and looked away. Doctor Morelle was bent over the figure on the couch.

'Bullet in the heart,' he murmured. 'Death must have been instantaneous.'

Miss Frayle was looking at an attractive young woman who had edged into a corner of the dressing room as they entered. The stage-manager had spoken to her solicitously, and Miss Frayle had recognised her as the actress who had fired the revolver. She was staring at the Doctor with a face that was distraught. Obviously tears had played havoc with her make-up. Miss Frayle noticed tiny black daubs around her eyes where the mascara had run.

'It's terrible . . . terrible!' she sobbed.

'Please, Miss Carson . . . Please.'

The stage-director moved over to her and patted her shoulders clumsily. The young woman sank into a chair and sobbed into a handkerchief. The other looked at her in blank helplessness, then crossed over to the Doctor.

'What — what are we going to do?' he muttered hopelessly.

Doctor Morelle glanced up with a

saturnine expression.

'No doubt a solution to the problem will present itself,' he murmured enigmatically. Miss Frayle gave him a quick look, and was about to speculate on the meaning that lay behind his remark, when a tall, heavily-built man wearing an evening tailcoat came bustling into the room. He wore a gardenia in his buttonhole, and also an air of great importance. He glanced at the stage-director who indicated the Doctor. The newcomer went over, to recoil with a gasp as he glimpsed at the dead actor.

'My God!' he exclaimed.

Doctor Morelle eyed him quizzically.

'I'm Pemberton,' the man said, fingering his white tie. 'Maurice Pemberton. I'm the manager of the theatre.' He paused, and then, as the Doctor merely made a grave inclination of the head, went on: 'This is a shocking business! What's — er — what's to be done about it?'

'I should imagine your first step would be to inform the audience that the performance cannot continue.'

The other nodded. 'In view of all this . . . Yes, I agree.' He spoke crisply. He glanced at the stage-manager, then at the actress who was quieter now. 'Yes,' he said decisively, 'I'd better go and tell them . . . ' He turned abruptly on his heel and went quickly towards the door.

Doctor Morelle murmured: 'You are, of course, aware that the police must be notified?' Pemberton stopped as if he had been struck, and stared at him. The actress looked up with a startled face.

'Police!' she gasped. 'They won't think I did it? I didn't know it was really loaded . . . '

Pemberton went over to her.

'Now, now, my dear Mary, pull yourself together!' He turned to the stage-manager. 'I think you'd better see Miss Carson to her own dressing room.'

'Let me take care of her.' It was Miss Frayle who came quickly forward and took the young woman's arm. 'Take a sniff at these smelling salts,' she coaxed her, and led her out of the room. Mary Carson had started to cry again, and as the sounds of sobbing receded the stage-manager carefully closed the door.

Pemberton stood in a thoughtful attitude. He appeared to be considering Doctor Morelle's last remark.

'I suppose we've no alternative but to 'phone the police,' he muttered dubiously.

'Nasty business. Damned unpleasant publicity.' The Doctor, eyeing him shrewdly, found no difficulty in discerning he was weighing up the affair almost entirely from the angle of the effect it might have upon the receipts at the box-office of his theatre.

'Will you wait here, Doctor, while I go and make that announcement?' he said. 'Then we'll 'phone the police from my office in the front of the house.'

'Very well.'

With a nod the other went out briskly. The Doctor took an inevitable Le Sphinx from his cigarette case and flicked his lighter. The stage-manager, who remained behind, looked at him uncertainly. Then he took down a sheet that was used to protect the actor's clothes hanging on the wall from face-powder dust, and covered the dead man with it. Doctor Morelle watched him in silence. The man said, after a moment:

'Shocking thing for Miss Carson. I think she was, well — rather keen on him.'

'Indeed!'

'Yes,' the other mused. 'Take her a bit of time to get over it, I'm afraid. Firing the revolver and everything. Terrible for her.'

Doctor Morelle blew a puff of cigarette smoke towards the ceiling. He watched it spread and disintegrate into the atmosphere with an abstracted gaze.

'Poor old Gerald Winters, too,' the other was saying. 'Final curtain for him all right.' He sighed heavily.

'That is a remarkably fine glass eye you have,' Doctor Morelle observed suddenly.

The other gaped at him in surprise.

'Why yes,' he stammered. 'You — er — you're one of the few people who've noticed it.'

'My powers of observation are not unexceptional!' The Doctor gave him a complacent smile. There was a moment's silence. Then he went on: 'So you are the

— ah — stage-manager, did you not say?'

'That's right.'

'You've no doubt examined the firearm Miss Carson used tonight?'

'Certainly. Grabbed it and had a look at it soon as I knew something had gone wrong.' A thought struck him, and he pulled a revolver from his pocket. Doctor Morelle noticed it was carefully wrapped in a silk handkerchief.

'This is the gun.'

The Doctor took the revolver and, holding it carefully, snapped open the breech.

'It would appear that a live cartridge has been substituted for a blank,' he said at length.

The other nodded.

'I've seen nobody else has touched it.' Then he added: 'In case the police want to test it for fingerprints.'

Doctor Morelle inclined his head in approval. He rewrapped the gun in the handkerchief and returned it to the man.

'As the stage-manager, you would be responsible for this?'

'Yes, I take charge of it — see it's okay

before the curtain gocs up, then pass it on to Miss Carson. After the second act, she gives it back to me, and I load it up again, ready for the next show.'

'You keep a container of blank cartridges specially for the purpose?'

'That's right. In a box.'

'You always load the firearm in a good light? There would be no chance of a live cartridge, providing one had in some manner found its way into the container, escaping your notice?'

The other shook his head emphatically. 'Not a chance!'

Their conversation was interrupted by the return of Maurice Pemberton.

'Well, that's that,' he declared as he shut the door after him. 'Now I suppose we get the police.'

The Doctor tapped the ash off his cigarette.

'I would like a word with Miss Carson before you do that,' he suggested.

'Certainly.' He turned to the stage-manager. 'Better wait around, Denning,' he said, 'just in case.'

'Right.'

Mary Carson's dressing room was two doors along the corridor. They found she had recovered her composure to the extent of removing her stage make-up. She was in the process of putting on her ordinary make-up, and was chatting to Miss Frayle when they entered. Pemberton took her hand and patted it sympathetically.

'We all know how you feel, dear,' he told her. 'Try to bear up. There'll be no more show for tonight, so just you get home and make an effort to get some sleep. Doctor Morelle here wants to ask you a question or two.' He added: 'No doubt if you feel you'll need it, he'll give you something to make you sleep.'

'I think Miss Carson's feeling better,' put in Miss Frayle.

Doctor Morelle chose a chair that had the strong lights of the mirror as much as possible behind him.

'Concerning the firearm used by you, Miss Carson,' he began smoothly. 'I understand it is brought to you every evening?'

'Yes,' she said slowly. 'Jim Denning always brings it along to my dressing room himself. I leave it here on the dressing table, ready for my entrance just before the shooting scene.'

'I understand. I assume you are out of your dressing room from time to time?'

'Of course.'

'During the time between it being left with you and your taking it with you on to the stage, could anyone else have access to it?'

She thought for a moment. She said:

'It would be very difficult for anyone to tamper with it without being seen.'

'You would appear to be somewhat positive on that point.'

'Well, you see,' she explained, 'until the end of the second act, Gerald and I never meet in the play. As he makes his exit, I go on — and vice versa.'

'I remember noticing that,' corroborated Miss Frayle. Doctor Morelle directed a look of irritation at her, and she subsided.

'When I'm on the stage, and Gerald's in his dressing room, he always kept his door open, so's he could hear me and judge his cue. He never relied on the call-boy.'

'Your suggestion is, then, that no one could have entered this room in your absence without being observed by the deceased?'

'Nobody . . . ' Her voice broke and she choked: 'Oh, poor Gerald!'

'Need you ask her any more questions?' put in Miss Frayle with an anxious look at Mary Carson. The Doctor turned on her, his eyes narrowed ill-temperedly.

'Why, do you mind?' he queried with excessive solicitude.

'Well, don't you think that perhaps Miss Carson — ' She broke off under his baleful stare.

Pemberton, with a look at the actress, who seemed distressed and about to break down once more, said hurriedly: 'I think Doctor, perhaps she isn't quite up to answering a lot of questions — '

He was interrupted by the door opening. A man stood there looking at them uncertainly. He was a slim young man and Mary Carson turned to him with a cry.

'Oh, my dear — !'

'Can I come in?' And the newcomer

came in, pushing the door closed. He spoke in quick, clipped phrases.

'How ghastly about Gerald!'

Mary Carson turned to the Doctor and Miss Frayle.

'This is my brother ... ' She introduced them.

He gave them both a quick look. Then: 'You're the doctor, are you?'

'Good evening.' Doctor Morelle replied suavely.

'Always thought that gun was dangerous!' he rattled on. To Pemberton: 'Remember? On the first night, I said to you: 'Bet you'll have an accident with that damned gun!' Remember? Too realistic!'

He turned to his sister: 'You poor darling! How frightful for you.'

Pemberton said: 'Mary's suffering from shock, Mr. Carson.'

'I can't believe it's happened.' She drew a hand across her face and shuddered.

Carson blurted out: 'Suppose it sounds rottenly callous and all that — but, well — it's a bit of a blow to me, too.' He hesitated as if deciding whether he should continue, then went on: 'Gerald owed me five hundred — '

'Oh, please — !' Mary Carson looked up at him appealingly.

'Sorry, old thing,' he apologised. 'But he was up to the neck in debt all round.' No one spoke. Doctor Morelle's thoughts seemed far away. Carson mumbled: 'Ah, well . . . poor chap.'

The atmosphere of embarrassment he had caused as a result of his talkativeness was relieved by the entrance of the stage-director.

'I've told no one to leave the theatre, Mr. Pemberton,' he said, 'until the police have given them permission. Is that right?'

The other nodded. 'Right, Denning — By Jove! I'd better get on to them, too,' he exclaimed. 'Doctor Morelle, perhaps you'd care to come along with me to my office while I telephone Scotland Yard?'

'As you wish. Miss Frayle, you will remain here.'

'Yes, Doctor.'

Mary Carson whispered brokenly: 'Will they want to question me?'

'I'm afraid so,' murmured Doctor Morelle.

'Oh . . . Oh! I can't bear it — '

'Please try and keep calm,' Miss Frayle said quietly. 'It'll be all right.'

'It — it's like a nightmare — ' the young woman choked.

Her brother patted her shoulder ineffectually. 'I say, try and take it easy, old dear.'

Doctor Morelle said to Miss Frayle from the door: 'This, Miss Frayle, should provide you with an opportunity to observe police procedure — when the authorities arrive — at close quarters. A unique experience!' And with a saturnine glance at her, he went out.

A few minutes later in Pemberton's office, he lit a Le Sphinx and observed as the manager picked up the telephone:

'It would considerably facilitate matters if you asked to speak personally to Detective-Inspector Hood. That is, in the event of that officer being there at this hour.'

Pemberton looked at him somewhat questioningly.

'I have some acquaintance with the Detective-Inspector,' he condescended to explain through a cloud of cigarette smoke. 'Merely mention my name and he will react with appropriate despatch.'

The other spoke into the telephone. As it happened he was able to catch the Detective-Inspector just as he was leaving for his home. Pemberton gave him the message as he had been instructed by the Doctor, and Hood promised to come along to the theatre immediately. Replacing the receiver, Pemberton regarded Doctor Morelle with an expression of new and profound respect, which was accepted with a typically self-satisfied and bleakly humorous smile.

'While we are awaiting the arrival of the Scotland Yard representative,' he murmured to the theatre manager, 'you might supply me with the answers to one or two questions I should like to ask.'

'Certainly — if you think I can,' replied Pemberton, pinching the end off a cigar and carefully lighting it.

'I am under the distinct impression,' said Doctor Morelle smoothly, 'that those who have so far vouchsafed any information concerning the unfortunate incident tonight have contrived to remain suspiciously reticent.'

The other's cigar was halted abruptly half way to his mouth. 'You mean, you think that — ?'

'If we might confine ourselves to facts and omit attempts at surmise in terms of generalities,' the Doctor interrupted him with an imperious wave of his hand. 'Tell me,' he went on suavely, examining the tip of his cigarette with elaborate interest, 'are you aware that the deceased had incurred the enmity of any person?'

The other seemed puzzled.

'Well, I don't know,' he said slowly. 'Gerald Winters was a pretty decent chap. I liked him. There may have been one or two who didn't — professional jealousy, perhaps, and all that. But — '

'But no one was, to your knowledge, sufficiently antagonistic towards him to perform an act of homicide?'

'Oh, no, I'm quite sure not.'

There was a brief silence. Then Doctor Morelle observed casually: 'It will be wiser for you to let me have all the information — however, irrelevant it may seem to you — concerning either Miss Carson or Gerald Winters.' He added significantly: 'Or both.'

Pemberton shot him a wary glance. He hesitated a moment, shrugged his shoulders and pulled at his cigar thoughtfully.

'You might as well know . . . ' he said slowly. 'The first point is that a year or two ago, Gerald Winters and the Carson girl had a pretty hectic love affair.' He paused. Doctor Morelle made no comment.

'Well,' the other went on, 'you've seen her tonight. Daresay gathered she's a superficial sort of creature. Rather like her acting, I suppose, effective within a certain range, but lacking in depth of character. So it may not be much of a surprise to you to know — it certainly didn't surprise their friends! — that she began to get tired of Winters. And the man to whom she transferred her attentions was another actor as he then was, named Jim Denning.'

'Denning?' The Doctor's eyebrows shot up.

'Yes — the stage-director you met

tonight. Well, Gerald Winters was fiercely possessive about Mary Carson, not unnaturally, and it so happened that at the time he and Denning were both attending the same fencing school — lots of actors go in for it in case they might appear in a costume play — and rumour has it that one day they fought a sort of unofficial duel over Miss Carson. Anyhow, that's how Denning lost an eye. Perhaps you didn't notice he wears a glass eye.'

Doctor Morelle chose to ignore the last remark with the contempt he considered it deserved. Pemberton went on:

'The whole business was hushed up, Denning himself swore it was an accident. But that wasn't the end of it. Anyway, Mary Carson went back to Winters — for a time. She chucked him altogether after a few months.'

'Do you think Denning might harbour malice?' asked Doctor Morelle. 'Men of his type — the quiet, introspective mentality — sometimes do. It would appear that to substitute a live cartridge in the revolver would be a comparatively easy matter for him.'

The theatre manager surveyed the glowing tip of his cigar, with a thoughtful air.

'I must say I *had* viewed the matter in that light,' he confessed. 'There may be something in what you say. Though, personally, I'd never have considered Denning a vindictive chap. After all, he was decent and generous enough over the duel. Losing an eye is no laughing matter for an actor . . . In his case he felt he couldn't continue in the theatre — except on the technical side.'

Doctor Morelle said:

'Did Winters marry someone else in due course?'

'Yes, two years ago. I believe they've been very happy. I don't think Mary Carson's ever married. And that's about all I can tell you of their private lives. Sure you won't have a drink?'

Doctor Morelle shook his head. The other poured himself a generous whisky and soda.

'I suppose it was risky to have had them in the same play together,' he said as he took a drink. 'Never trust women when they come up against old flames! Eh, Doctor Morelle — ?' His expression changed. 'That reminds me,' he said suddenly. He appeared to be trying to recall something from the depths of his memory.

The Doctor eyed him narrowly.

'It was this afternoon,' Pemberton said slowly. 'After the matinée I happened to be backstage, and heard a dressing room door open — either Gerald Winters' or hers — and I got the tail-end of a conversation. It sounded like a bit of a quarrel — the voices were loud — I couldn't help hearing him say something about: 'I tell you I can't do it — I'm up to my eyes in debt, thanks to you.' Yes, that was it . . . Then she said: 'I'll give you till tomorrow!' Then the door slammed, one of them must have come out. It didn't occur to me to see who it was. I was pretty busy at the time, didn't think very much about it. I supposed one of them had probably been lending the other money or something, and — ' He broke off with a shrug.

'What you have told me opens up an

interesting avenue for speculation,' Doctor Morelle murmured.

'In a way, though, it clears Mary Carson,' the other pointed out. 'That is, if there was any suspicion against her. I mean, she gave him till tomorrow to repay this money, or whatever it was, so she'd hardly have wanted to kill him tonight!'

The Doctor gave him a non-committal glance. He said:

'Alternatively it postulates the possibility of another and rather more subtle crime.'

Maurice Pemberton was appreciably startled.

'Good God! This is getting a bit involved!' He hesitated, then asked; 'Will it be necessary for the police to go into all this?'

'You may rely upon me to offer Detective-Inspector Hood just as much of the information I have elicited as I deem expedient for the purpose of accelerating the wheels of justice,' Doctor Morelle replied with enigmatic suaveness.

The theatre-manager looked at him sharply. He was taking a hurried gulp of whisky when there was a rap on the door.

With a nervous glance at the Doctor, he called out: 'Come in!'

It was Detective-Inspector Hood who stood in the doorway.

★　★　★

At the house in Harley Street some two or three, hours later, Detective-Inspector Hood was being served coffee by Miss Frayle. They were in the study, and he was saying to the Doctor who was leaning casually against his desk: 'Never like dealing with these artistic people. Always try to make you, and themselves for that matter, believe they're what they're not.' He shook his head. 'Perhaps it's all in the nature of their work, as you might say!'

He sipped his coffee.

'However . . . ' he went on cheerfully, and thrust a hand into a pocket to produce a tiny object that he held out for the Doctor's inspection. Miss Frayle watched Doctor Morelle gaze at it through a cloud of cigarette smoke with interest.

Hood was saying: 'I made a pretty

thorough search of the dressing rooms. Found that behind the dressing table mirror in Miss Carson's room.'

Miss Frayle goggled at the small unexploded blank cartridge which lay in the palm of the Doctor's hand. He returned it to the detective.

'Too small to register a clear finger-print,' he murmured.

'Yes.'

'Then I don't quite see how it can help very much,' put in Miss Frayle.

Doctor Morelle eyed her superciliously.

'You amaze me, my dear Miss Frayle!' He turned to Hood and went on: 'It merely confirms my theory, however, that the person responsible entered Miss Carson's dressing room during her absence on the stage, and substituted a live cartridge for this blank.'

'Unless, of course, she did it herself,' Hood said over his cup of coffee.

The Doctor regarded him with a saturnine smile. 'If you can supply a convincing reason why Miss Carson should choose to murder Winters before a theatre full of people your suggestion might be worthy of consideration.'

The Detective-Inspector thought for a moment.

'That is a bit of a poser,' he admitted heavily. 'Of course, she's tough enough. Got plenty of guts. Might have thought she could get away with it — '

'But the motive?' Doctor Morelle persisted.

'Yes, why should she do that — ?' began Miss Frayle, but he waved her into silence.

'You've got me there, Doctor. According to Pemberton, they'd had a bit of an argument in the afternoon. About money or something. But these actors are always going up in the air over something!'

'I would make the suggestion that you interview the one non-artistic person involved in the case. I refer to Mrs. Winters, the deceased's wife.'

The other nodded. 'Seeing her first thing in the morning.' He put down his empty cup and produced a pipe. 'Well, I'll be getting back to the theatre, I suppose. Still got plenty of routine stuff to check.'

At the front door he said:

'You like to talk to Mrs. Winters with me, Doctor?'

Doctor Morelle said with studied disinterest: 'If you wish.'

Hood grinned at him. He knew the Doctor would have harboured it as a grievance against him forever had he omitted to invite him along.

'Fine! Collect you nineish . . . Goodnight . . . Goodnight, Miss Frayle!'

★   ★   ★

Mrs. Winters proved to be a sturdily good-looking young woman with a firm grip on herself, and obviously determined not to break down under the stress of the tragedy which had befallen her.

She said, in answer to one of the Detective-Inspector's questions:

'He always said that if ever anything happened to him I was to go to the Central Bank — the branch office nearby — and see the manager. I haven't had time to give it a thought yet.'

Hood nodded sympathetically.

'You haven't been to the bank?' It was

187

Doctor Morelle who sought a definite statement.

'No, not yet.'

The detective's skilful questioning, together with one or two shrewd queries from Doctor Morelle had elicited the following:

Gerald Winters had been leading a comfortable life, happily married to all appearances, and, it seemed, just about to achieve success of a more outstanding nature in the theatre. He owned an expensive car, and his wife had only recently returned from a holiday at a fashionable resort. She wore expensive-looking clothes of excellent taste. On the surface there appeared to be nothing that could be associated with a reason for his death.

Doctor Morelle suggested to his companion that he had sensed, however, an indefinable feeling of insecurity and instability about the atmosphere of the Winters' home. They were quitting the opulently architectured building in which the flat they had been visiting was situated as the Doctor made this observation.

'I agree,' said Hood. 'Something wrong there, though you can't put your finger on it.' He sighed heavily. 'Well . . . what next?'

'Might we not pay a visit to the Central Bank, while we are in the vicinity?' insinuated Doctor Morelle.

On the Scotland Yard official producing his authority, they were ushered into the bank manager's office. The manager was a plump little individual with an ingratiating manner. He seemed more anxious to chat to them on generalities than he was to reveal anything concerning his client's account. Detective-Inspector Hood was very firm, however.

'I merely want a little advance information on a matter which will have to be revealed to Somerset House in due course,' he said. 'Of course, if you prefer it, my Chief can get in touch with your Chairman . . . '

The plump little man seemed to make up his mind at last. He coughed delicately, glanced quickly at the detective and then at Doctor Morelle.

'Very well, Inspector, what exactly did

you want to know?' he said.

'First of all, is Gerald Winters' account overdrawn?'

'It most certainly is,' was the straight-forward answer. 'I telephoned him the other day, as a matter of fact, to advise him that his account was in a condition such as could no longer be permitted to continue.'

'Had you no security?' queried Doctor Morelle quietly.

The man smiled slightly. 'It is not the practice of the bank to advance loans without security. Mr. Winters deposited with us a life policy. Quite a large policy — a matter of seven thousand pounds in the event of his death.'

'Might I peruse the policy in question?'

The manager looked inquiringly at the Doctor, then quizzed Hood, who nodded his confirmation of the request. The other spoke into his private telephone. In a few moments the policy was brought in. While the manager chatted agreeably with the Inspector, Doctor Morelle read the document through, clause by clause. Presently, with a smirk of self-satisfaction, he returned it.

The manager said, placing the document in his desk:

'I'd had a talk previously with Mr. Winters in this office only a few weeks ago. He wanted me to increase his limit. He'd been borrowing from friends, it appeared, and wished to repay them. I fear I gave him quite a lecture — in a friendly way, of course!' He spread his plump hands expressively. 'These artistic people seem to have no sense of proportion where money is concerned! D'you know I believe they regard it simply as something to spend . . . '

★   ★   ★

In the police car which was dropping Doctor Morelle at Harley Street before proceeding on to Scotland Yard, Detective-Inspector Hood sucked a cold pipe and grumbled:

'Well . . . Been a pretty wasted morning, I must say!'

The Doctor made no reply. His eyes

were closed. Hood glanced at him, wondering if he had not fallen asleep. His eyelids flickered momentarily and then closed again. The detective said:

'I don't see how anything we've discovered helps us an inch further.'

'On the contrary,' murmured Doctor Morelle in an almost somnolent tone, 'it has furnished us with precisely the information we seek.'

Hood stared at him.

'How d'you mean?' he asked with a puzzled frown.

'I refer to the missing motive,' the Doctor said as he took a Le Sphinx from his case and lit it. 'If you would care to stop at my residence for a brief while, I will amplify my statement accordingly. You will then be able to proceed directly to Scotland Yard with a complete report upon this somewhat unusual case.'

The detective laughed admiringly.

'All right, Doctor, I have to hand it to you!' And he gave the policeman at the wheel appropriate instructions.

A little while later Doctor Morelle, in his most condescending mood was sitting back in his chair listening to the sound of his own voice with ill-concealed self-satisfaction.

'Motive,' he was saying, his gaze flickering from Detective-Inspector Hood to Miss Frayle and back again, both of whom were hanging on his words with suitably awe-inspired expressions. 'That was the key to the mystery of Gerald Winters' mysterious demise.'

He paused, flicked the ash off his cigarette and went on in the same pompous and yet curiously fascinating tone that held his listeners' attention.

'It was Miss Carson's brother who first suggested to me — inadvertently, needless to say — that motive might be the vital clue which would lead to the elucidation of the problem. You may recall the remark the young man passed to the effect that the deceased owed him money and was in fact deeply in debt? That remark prompted me to consider a theory which — ah — ' he smiled indulgently ' — had so far escaped attention.'

He blew a cloud of cigarette smoke through his finely chiselled nostrils. He said:

'That theory was based on an obvious if not immediately apparent fact: The one person who could benefit by the tragedy was the chief actor in it. In other words, Winters himself!'

He paused dramatically. Miss Frayle obligingly filled in the gap of silence with a gasp of admiring amazement. He rewarded her with a patronising smile.

'His demise,' he went on, 'covered — as was subsequently revealed to be the case — as it was by an insurance policy, would relieve him in every sense from financial difficulties and leave his dependants, his wife in particular, secure.'

Hood interjected: 'But why go to all that trouble? Slipping into Mary Carson's dressing room, substituting the cartridge, and all that?'

'Because,' Doctor Morelle almost stifled a yawn at what he regarded as the other's dullness, 'the insurance policy in question contained a clause. A clause that declared the policy void in the event of the holder committing *felo-de-se*. Winters' problem, therefore, was to stage his death in such a way that it would not appear self-inflicted.

He hit upon the ingenious plan of having himself shot as the result of an 'accident'.'

'You mean he really committed suicide?' Miss Frayle goggled at him through her spectacles.

'Precisely, my *dear* Miss Frayle!' the Doctor said with heavy sarcasm.

The detective scratched his head. 'Beats me where people get their ideas from!' he said at length.

Doctor Morelle regarded him thoughtfully for a moment.

'I am constrained to wonder that myself,' he murmured softly, 'on occasion!'

And with this ambiguous observation he stubbed out his cigarette with an air that conveyed that for him, at any rate, the case he had elucidated so simply could now be considered closed.

7

THE CASE OF THE
INTERRUPTED TELEPHONE CALL

Miss Frayle said, as she came into the study:

'What have you been saying to poor Inspector Hood? He looked quite upset as he went out.'

She blinked interrogatively at the Doctor who had settled himself again at his desk and was scanning a file of papers. He made no reply to her question, but went on reading as if oblivious of her presence. She gave him a reproachful glance and busied herself checking the last few pages of a voluminous notebook. Silence fell on the study, except for the occasional rustle of a paper or document. From outside came the muffled hum of the evening traffic passing up and down Harley Street.

It was several weeks after Doctor

Morelle had solved the strange mystery of Gerald Winters' tragic death during the performance of London's most popular horror-play. The Doctor had almost forgotten Detective-Inspector Hood's existence, though he had been reminded of him on occasion when passing the theatre at which the tragedy had occurred. For he had observed with sardonic mirth which, in his case, passed for humour, that the horror-play, with another actor in the role Gerald Winters had so tragically vacated, was playing to packed audiences. Maurice Pemberton, manager of the theatre, had calculatingly taken full advantage of the publicity the play had attracted as a result of the dramatic circumstances surrounding Winters' death.

It was somewhat of a surprise to him, therefore, when Miss Frayle had earlier that evening informed him Detective-Inspector Hood was on the telephone asking for an appointment as soon as possible. Having a comparatively free half-hour at that time, the Doctor had invited the detective along whenever he wished, and the latter had left his office at once. The ensuing interview occupied only a few minutes and the sturdy Detective-Inspector had taken his leave, sucking his pipe noisily and with only the barest glimmer of a smile for Miss Frayle as he left.

Miss Frayle looked up from her notebook as Doctor Morelle gave a little murmur that might have indicated puzzlement. It was the sort of murmur she found difficult to associate with him. He glanced at her through narrowed lids and rose to his feet. He took a cigarette from the skull cigarette box and lit it thoughtfully. He gave a little cough and cleared his throat. She looked at him expectantly. Satisfied she was all attention, he spoke:

'I have always been at a loss to comprehend,' he said in slightly pained tones, 'how anyone could at any time be actuated by a feeling of dislike towards me.'

Miss Frayle goggled at him.

He paused and regarded her as if expecting an immediate answer. She strove heroically to think of something to say.

'Why, Doctor, has anyone ever told you they disliked you?' was all she could hit on. And then added judiciously: 'I wonder why?'

He said with calm seriousness:

'I could only conclude it was merely a matter of their jealous envy of my obvious talents.'

She was by now, of course, more than used to his moods of overbearing egotism and merely said:

'You mean people who didn't like you really wished they could be as you were?' (For a horrified moment she wondered if she had not even for him laid it on a bit too thick. But he appeared to accept her question as being completely in the nature of things. There was no doubt, the thought flashed through her mind, when at a loss, just tell him he's wonderful!)

He was answering her spoken query.

'Precisely. A psychological trait not uncommon in characters of lesser quality — ' Suddenly he broke off to observe in a dangerously level tone: 'Did I detect, my dear Miss Frayle, a suggestion in your question of derisive sarcasm?' She caught her breath, gulped and only just managed to blurt out:

'Oh no, Doctor Morelle, of course not! You have all my sympathy.'

He stared at her through the smoke of his Le Sphinx. Then he said: 'Hmmm . . . I feel a little less sympathy and more application to your work would make a greater appeal to me!' And he returned to his desk. She could not restrain a feeling of some amusement at the way she had been congratulating herself upon her cleverness, only to learn as she always did that he was never on any occasion to be deceived.

'And kindly remove that irritating simper from your face!' he snapped at her across the room.

She was about to sigh when the telephone rang. She answered it.

'This is Doctor Morelle's house,' she said.

She could plainly hear over the wire heavy, distressed breathing. As if the caller was terribly agitated and in great haste.

'The Doctor!' a man's voice gasped. 'I must speak to him! It's a matter of life and death! Quick — I must speak to him!'

'Who are you, please?'

'Never mind who I am — ! Get me the Doctor — I must speak — !'

'Who is it, Miss Frayle? What do they want?'

Doctor Morelle had snapped the query without looking up from his desk. She glanced at him helplessly.

'It's some man, Doctor,' she stammered. 'I don't know who he is — he won't say — '

With an exclamation of impatience he was beside her.

'This is Doctor Morelle,' he snapped into the telephone. 'Who are you?'

'Doctor — ?' The voice seemed to give a sob of relief. Then it babbled on: 'This is a friend. Listen! You're in danger. Jim Carver's out to do for you!' The voice rose higher. 'Don't go to Orient Wharf!'

Doctor Morelle's eyebrows shot up in surprise.

'Orient Wharf? Carver? Who — ?'

'You got his brother a stretch!' came the succinct explanation. The voice went on:

'I tell you Carver's going to trick you down to Bridge House, Orient Wharf, and — '

'From where are you telephoning?' the Doctor cut in.

'A call-box in River Street. You've got to believe me, Doctor! You've got to — !'

Suddenly the voice at the other end of the wire broke off. The man spoke now in a horrified whisper.

'He — he's coming along the street! He's seen me — !' Again the voice broke off. It rose again in what was almost a scream: 'My God! He's got a gun — ! Carver's got a gun — !'

There was the sound of a revolver shot, a tinkle of glass, a choking cough. Then silence.

Doctor Morelle depressed the receiver rest rapidly.

'Hello? Hello . . . ?'

Miss Frayle was at his side, her spectacles slipping on her nose in excitement.

'Doctor Morelle!' she gasped breathlessly. 'What happened? It sounded like a shot!'

'It was a shot!' he snapped, and replaced the receiver. He stubbed out his cigarette. He moved quickly to the door.

'Where are you going?'

He spoke over his shoulder. 'To an urban thoroughfare known, I understand, as River Street. If you wish to accompany me you had better accelerate your reflexes and at the same time restrain your spectacles from being precipitated to the floor!' And he was out of the room.

Grabbing her recalcitrant lenses just in time, Miss Frayle shot after him. In the taxi she asked him:

'Didn't you mention the name Carver over the telephone? Wasn't that the name of the man who was sent to prison for blackmail?'

'The answer to both your questions is identical and in the affirmative,' he informed her in a tone of mock gravity. 'It was directly as a result of my activities on behalf of a patient that a certain Richard Thornton Carver received a term of penal servitude.'

River Street, they discovered, was a branch off one of the innumerable byways leading from the Limehouse Road. It was a cul-de-sac with the River Thames at one end, and already a thin curtain of evening mist was muffled round the gaunt warehouses and derricks that hemmed in the dark and somewhat forbidding-looking street. Miss Frayle shivered as Doctor Morelle instructed the driver to stop on the corner and she got out. He paid off the taxi and it disappeared into the gloom. She followed him, glancing apprehensively about her, as he moved briskly off.

'It — it's all rather sinister, don't you think?' she shuddered.

'You must take a grip on that imagination of yours, Miss Frayle,' he snapped. 'I am acutely aware this is not exactly a salubrious district, but there are doubtless many worse neighbour-hoods.'

'I find it hard to believe!' she said, quickening her pace to keep up with him.

'This that we are now approaching is, no doubt, the telephone-box I wish to investigate.' He indicated a call-box which stood on the corner of an entrance to an alleyway between the buildings.

'Yes — look — !' she cried. 'The

window's broken — that would be by the shot!'

She indicated a small hole drilled in the side of the box. It was about shoulder-high. Doctor Morelle produced a narrow torch and picked out several — tiny splinters of glass on the pavement outside. He opened the call-box door and shone his torch inside.

'H'm the body would seem to have vanished!'

Miss Frayle glanced at him questioningly. He had spoken in a voice that betrayed no surprise. The telephone receiver had been replaced on its hook.

'What could have happened to him?' she asked.

He made no reply, but bent and examined the floor carefully. Straightening himself after a moment, he observed:

'Unfortunately, he failed signally to leave any clue behind . . . The floor is perfectly clean, as you will perceive.' He gave the shelf that held the telephone a cursory look, and shook the directory. Nothing appeared to excite his interest.

'There's a funny smell, Doctor!' Miss

Frayle was sniffing the atmosphere inside the box suspiciously. 'It's like a strong cigar.'

He permitted himself a mirthless smile.

'It would be a potent weed indeed which contained the ingredients producing that aroma!'

She looked at him sharply.

'What d'you mean?'

'Merely that it happens to be the odour of nitroglycerine plus nitrocellulose, explosive components of gunpowder.'

'Oh,' she said, with an expression of appropriate enlightenment, 'I see . . . '

'On the contrary,' he flashed back at her, 'you are exercising your olfactory senses!'

Miss Frayle realised she was sniffing like an over-zealous retriever puppy and subsided. From the river a tug's siren hooted dismally. The mist swirled eerily about them. The Doctor seemed oblivious of his surroundings, however. Lighting a cigarette he stepped into the street, the door slamming behind. The flame of his lighter illuminated his saturnine features for a brief moment. His eyes were dark and speculative under the brim of his hat. Miss Frayle coughed as the fog caught her throat. With a shiver she hunched her shoulders into her coat.

'Do you think the man Carver's taken the — er — body to the place at Orient Wharf you said he mentioned on the telephone?'

He gave her a glance of studied admiration.

'Miss Frayle, your genius for perceiving the obvious positively overwhelms me!'

'Well, hadn't we better go there?' she suggested impatiently. 'He may be only wounded, and we might save him.'

'You possess a quixotically chivalrous nature,' he murmured sardonically. But he made no move. He stood flashing his torch in the immediate vicinity of the box as if in search of something.

'Well then, let's go, shall we?'

'A moment, however, before we tilt at windmills!' Opening the door of the call-box again, he stepped inside.

'What are you doing?'

'Merely ascertaining whether or not this telephone is in working order,' he said, operating the dial.

'Oh, but oughtn't we to hurry?'

'Hurry on, Donna Quixote!' he snapped. 'I will overtake you and accompany you with all speed to our destination.'

Goaded by his derisive tone, and feeling the necessity for some exercise to restore some warmth to her chilled limbs, she took him at his word. Slowly, however, and not without several backward glances, she proceeded along the street. Within a few moments his tall, gaunt figure loomed up out of the mist. She noticed his face wore a self-satisfied expression.

'Was it working?' she asked.

He glanced at her inquiringly.

'I beg your pardon?'

'The telephone. Was it in order?'

'Oh . . . Oh, yes! Eminently satisfactory,' he murmured abstractedly. He was obviously thinking of something quite different,

Bridge House proved to be a decrepit, rickety building which had, the Doctor deduced, at some time in the past been connected with one of the old bridges now demolished. It stood by itself on the edge of a wharf. Masses of decaying timbers blocked two sides of the building, and the back wall appeared to descend right into the river, where the gaunt outlines of a tramp steamer anchored not far distant loomed up black, its upper structure shrouded in the mist. The paint was peeling off the woodwork in the front of the place, and the windows were dirty and broken in places.

'Is — is this it?' Miss Frayle said dubiously.

'It would appear to be unoccupied,' murmured the Doctor. He stood back to survey the front of the building. Then moved to a doorway in the centre.

'The door is open slightly,' he said, 'so let us enter.'

The door squeaked complainingly as he pushed it back. He peered inside and looked round cautiously, allowing his eyes to grow accustomed to the gloom. Miss Frayle pressed close on his heels,

'Is — is it all right, Doctor?'

He turned and frowned at her obvious apprehension.

'Come, come, Miss Frayle, think of that poor suffering creature whom you are about to rescue!' he reminded her with heavy sarcasm.

He went in, his torch making a wandering pool of light on the walls. She followed him.

'It's very dark,' she shivered. The door creaked back to its semi-closed position behind her.

'The building seems at one time to have been a store place,' mused Doctor Morelle, noting several sacks in a corner and a number of empty crates. The light from his torch caught a ladder almost facing them. Evidently it led up to a loft.

'Would — would there be any rats?' came Miss Frayle's timid small voice.

'That we shall no doubt ascertain in due course!' he said, his sardonic tone giving her but cold comfort.

'Thank goodness you brought a torch — ' she began, and stopped with a gasp. There was a sound of scuffling in the darkness.

'Oh! What was that?'

'Merely your imagination! Follow me.

We will explore the upper regions.'

The ladder proved to be an insecure affair, and Miss Frayle clutched it grimly as she ascended shakily after the Doctor. He stood looking down from the opening in the loft at her clicking his tongue impatiently.

'Come along, Miss Frayle!'

'You might give me a hand,' she reproached him breathlessly, with a glance behind her. 'I — I thought I heard someone down there behind us.'

'Nonsense!' he snapped decisively. 'The place is empty!'

As he spoke there came a metallic click from behind him and an electric lamp was switched on. Its glow revealed a heavily-built man with a soft hat pulled down over his left eye. A jagged scar showed disfiguringly at one corner of his mouth, thrown into relief by his high cheekbones.

'Not exactly, Doctor Morelle!' the man jeered, coming forward menacingly.

'Oh, a man!' screamed Miss Frayle. 'Hold me — I'm falling!'

She clutched wildly at the darkness and

was in danger of falling backwards when Doctor Morelle reached down quickly. He gripped her shoulder and steadied her.

'You startled the young woman, appearing out of the shadows like that!' he observed coolly to the other.

The man laughed hoarsely: 'I'll startle her more before I've finished! And you too! Move over there — both of you!'

As Miss Frayle scrambled up beside the Doctor the stranger placed himself so as to cut off any chance they might have of retreating the way they had come. A wicked-looking automatic gleamed at them.

'Oh Doctor, he's got a gun!' Miss Frayle gasped unnecessarily.

'*And* it's liable to go off!' the man grinned. He waved them over away from the opening. He stood there himself and glanced down the ladder. Then he looked at them malevolently.

'Tricked you here nicely, didn't we Doctor Smartie?' he laughed.

'Morelle is the name.'

'I know who you are all right . . . And perhaps you'd care to know my name?'

'No doubt you would be Carver,' said the Doctor indifferently.

Miss Frayle caught her breath. The other stared at Doctor Morelle, a faint look of surprise showing in his face. Then he said:

'Yes . . . I'm Jim Carver. You may have heard of my brother?' he jeered; then he rasped: 'I swore I'd get you for what you did to him, and here you are, all to myself . . . with my pal keeping a lookout down below, so's we won't be interrupted!'

'What — what are you going to do with us?' gasped Miss Frayle.

'All in good time . . . When the tide's a bit higher,' and he nodded significantly. He said, with a grim chuckle: 'The river's nice and deep round here at full tide.'

Miss Frayle almost fainted with horror. She tried to tell herself it wasn't true. She'd wake up in a moment from some terrible nightmare. Doctor Morelle gave a little but somewhat ostentatious yawn. Still with his automatic menacing them, Carver shouted down the ladder:

'Everything okay down there, Eddie?'

'Oh, Doctor, we're caught!' Miss Frayle gulped. 'What will happen to us?' The Doctor did not even turn in her direction.

'Eddie!' Carver was calling again, a harsh note of impatience in his voice. 'Eddie — are you there?'

There was a sound of ascending footsteps on the ladder below.

'What are you coming up for?' snarled Carver. 'I told you to stay down there.'

The footsteps halted imperceptibly, then continued their upward journey. The man at the opening muttered, his expression puzzled.

Doctor Morelle said quietly:

'That, I regret to inform you, is Scotland Yard ascending the stepladder! Your friend — er — Eddie down below, has no doubt been quietly overpowered!'

Carver shot a disbelieving look at him, then, convinced by something in the Doctor's face, swung round and held his automatic pointed at the opening, As the footsteps came higher, Miss Frayle gave a sudden scream.

'Oh look — there's someone coming through that window!'

She was staring into the shadows directly behind Carver. He twisted his head to look.

The brisk voice of Detective-Inspector Hood hit him before he realised his mistake.

'Drop that gun, Carver! I've got you covered!' he warned him, his head and a revolver alone showing above the opening. Carver hesitated, his back to the detective.

'*Drop it!* And don't look round or I fire! Just drop the gun.' The automatic clattered to the floor. Doctor Morelle stepped forward and retrieved it, while Hood clambered into the loft. He was followed by three other determined-looking men who quickly took charge of Carver and led him below.

'Thanks, Miss Frayle,' the Detective-Inspector said gratefully. 'Neat of you to distract his attention like that. Everything in order, Doctor?'

The Doctor nodded and handed over the revolver.

'Our plan has worked with clockwork precision,' he replied. Miss Frayle gaped, first at the detective then at Doctor Morelle.

'Plan?' she echoed, completely mystified.

Detective-Inspector Hood chuckled at the expression on her face. He patted her arm and said: 'I expect the Doctor'll explain everything to you presently, Miss Frayle . . . '

But she was goggling at Doctor Morelle.

'Do you mean,' she said, 'you knew all along we were going to walk into this trap? And — and the police would come to our rescue?'

'Precisely, my dear Miss Frayle,' he smiled sardonically at the utter disbelief in her voice. He lit a cigarette and murmured with a sigh: 'Ah, me . . . I fear I am beginning to possess a somewhat suspicious nature!'

And with this enigmatic observation he motioned her to descend the ladder. Gingerly, her face still wearing a bewildered look, Miss Frayle began the descent.

★   ★   ★

In the study of the house in Harley Street some time later:

'On arrival at the telephone-box, in which, according to his description over the telephone, the caller who purported to be warning me of my danger was shot from outside, I at once perceived the man had been lying.'

Dutifully, Miss Frayle asked Doctor Morelle: 'How?'

The glow from the desk lamp added to the saturnine expression on his face as he went on with the air of addressing a small child.

'Because,' Doctor Morelle said, 'all the glass broken by the bullet had fallen on to the pavement. There was none on the floor inside the box. This, together with the presence within of gunpowder fumes was evidence that the revolver in question must have been fired inside the telephone-cubicle, and not from without.'

Miss Frayle nodded understandingly.

'And you mean,' she said, 'the whole business was arranged by that dreadful man Carver to — to lure you into a trap?'

'Precisely, Detective-Inspector Hood had warned me earlier that I was in some danger from the creature.' He smiled thinly. 'I fear I had not taken his warning seriously.'

She thought for a moment, then said:

'You got on to Scotland Yard, I suppose, when you told me you were testing the telephone to see if it still worked?'

He smiled thinly.

'That was the object of my little subterfuge.'

'Well . . . I think you might have warned me you were leading me into danger!' protested Miss Frayle.

He raised his eyebrows.

'My dear Miss Frayle!' he said suavely. 'I wished merely to offer you an opportunity to display those remarkable gifts of resourcefulness, any evidence of which you had up till then been withholding from me!'

She chose to hear only the first part of his remark. She said with a shy, pleased smile: 'You mean the way I made that awful man turn round so's he wouldn't shoot at Detective-Inspector Hood?' She made a deprecating movement with her hands. 'Oh . . . that was nothing.'

'Such a modest and unassuming young woman!' Doctor Morelle gave an ostentatious cough that made it palpably clear he was unconvinced. 'I suppose,' he said meaningfully, 'you did not for one moment imagine it really was someone climbing through the window behind Carver?'

Miss Frayle fidgeted uncomfortably.

Inexorably, that maddening sardonic voice insinuated:

'With your somewhat astigmatic vision, and in that shadowy light . . . '

Miss Frayle was blushing, and as he began to chuckle softly at her obvious discomfiture, tears of mortification blurred her spectacles. She blundered out of the study without pausing to say 'Goodnight'.

Doctor Morelle's mocking laughter followed her as she stumbled upstairs to bed.

THE END

DR. MORELLE MEETS MURDER
A CASE FOR DR. MORELLE
DR. MORELLE'S CASEBOOK
DR. MORELLE INVESTIGATES
DR. MORELLE INTERVENES
SEND FOR DR. MORELLE

We do hope that you have enjoyed reading this large print book.

Did you know that all of our titles are available for purchase?

We publish a wide range of high quality large print books including:
Romances, Mysteries, Classics
General Fiction
Non Fiction and Westerns

Special interest titles available in large print are:
The Little Oxford Dictionary
Music Book, Song Book
Hymn Book, Service Book

Also available from us courtesy of Oxford University Press:
Young Readers' Dictionary
(large print edition)
Young Readers' Thesaurus
(large print edition)

For further information or a free brochure, please contact us at:
Ulverscroft Large Print Books Ltd.,
The Green, Bradgate Road, Anstey,
Leicester, LE7 7FU, England.
Tel: (00 44) 0116 236 4325
Fax: (00 44) 0116 234 0205

THE STELLAR LEGION

E. C. Tubb

Wilson, a waif of the war of unity, spends his boyhood in forced labour. When he is sent to the penal world of Stellar, he survives, winning promotion in the Stellar Legion, a brutal military system. Laurance, Director of the Federation of Man, wants to dissolve the Legion. He pits his wits against its commander, Hogarth. He's terrified lest the human wolves, trained and hardened in blood and terror, should ravage the defenceless galaxy . . .

ENDLESS DAY

John Russell Fearn

It's June 30th. And in Annex 10, situated in the Adirondack Mountains of New York, scientist Dr. Gray and his team can hardly believe their instrument readings. It's four o'clock, and as the seconds pass, they see that chaos looms for mankind. The Earth is growing hotter, temperatures rocket, as the sun shines through the night and causes endless days. Everyone suffers — the rich, the poor, the criminal and the family man. Will it ever end?

EIGHT WEIRD TALES

Rafe McGregor

A curious woman investigates the dark secrets harboured within the ancient chapel of a ruined signal station. An antique ivory hunting horn will spell the downfall of Professor Goodspeed. Meanwhile, an eldritch voice draws a lonely man ever closer to the drowned town of Lod . . . Eight short tales, each directly inspired by a master of the mysterious or supernatural — Arthur Conan Doyle, H. P. Lovecraft, Anthony Hope, or M. R. James — which will send chills down your spine . . .